The woman printed out Chrissy's schedule in duplicate and set it on the counter. Thrilled to be done with the long registration process, Chrissy signed it quickly and took her copy. She was half way to the door when she realized her class schedule did not include the introductory course, Biology 101, but Biology 1001—Biogenetics and Ethics.

"Excuse me. There's a mistake in my schedule."

"Miss, it's not your turn," the woman said.

"Look at my schedule. I asked for Biology one-oh-one, but you put me in an advanced class. I can't take it—I'm just a freshman! Please fix it for me."

"No, I can't do that, " the woman responded firmly. "You'll have to transfer out of it on the first day of classes."

Chrissy pressed a damp palm to her forehead. *This is turning into a big nightmare,* she thought. *If only Caroline hadn't insisted on spending time with her new roommate, she'd be here right now to help me handle this awful situation . . .*

Other books in the **SUGAR & SPICE** series:

COMING SOON

Janet Quin-Harkin's
Sugar & Spice

Campus Cousins

IVY BOOKS • NEW YORK

Ivy Books
Published by Ballantine Books

Produced by Butterfield Press, Inc.
133 Fifth Avenue
New York, New York 10003

Library of Congress Catalog Card Number: 88-91245

ISBN: 0-8041-0335-6

Manufactured in the United States of America

First Edition: February 1989

Chapter 1

"Are those the Rocky Mountains?" Chrissy Madden leaned over the man in the window seat to get a better view.

The man sucked in his breath to give her more room. "The plane just took off half an hour ago," he explained. "We're probably somewhere over Nebraska."

"Nebraska?" Chrissy looked back at her neighbor. "I never knew they had mountains in Nebraska!"

"Let me see," said the man. After Chrissy moved back to her own seat, he peered out the small window. He turned to her with a smile. "Those aren't mountains—they're clouds in the distance."

"Really?" Chrissy asked in disbelief. She might

1

be from Danbury, Iowa, but she'd lived in San Francisco with her cousin Caroline Kirby for the past two years. Did this guy think she was some naive farm girl?

He simply nodded and pointed to what looked like snow-capped mountains on the horizon. "Your peaks are the tops of clouds, maybe even thunderheads. We must be flying at thirty thousand feet. Even the Rocky Mountains aren't that tall."

"You're right." Chrissy saw no reason to pretend she hadn't made a dumb mistake. "If the mountains were that high, the plane would collide with them!"

The man smiled. "Where are you headed?"

"Boulder," she told him proudly. "I'm going to be a freshman at Colorado University. I was on the waiting list, but finally I was admitted during the summer. I've *never* been so excited!"

"College . . ." he said. "I have a nephew who graduated from Colorado University last summer."

"Did he like it there?"

"It's an excellent school," he assured her. "Harper studied engineering, and now he's designing rockets."

"Holy mazoley! Rockets!" Under the seat, Chrissy kicked herself. She'd promised herself not to say such silly things now that she was going to be a college woman.

"What are you planning to study?" he asked.

"I have no idea," she admitted.

"Neither did my nephew," he confided. "You'll find out soon enough what interests you."

Chrissy grinned. That's exactly what she was hoping would happen. She was eighteen years old. How was she supposed to know what she wanted to do for her whole life? Wasn't that why she was going to college, anyway? College would be her chance to learn about the world and to decide what she wanted to be when she grew up.

Her neighbor opened his briefcase and started thumbing through papers. Since he seemed to be done talking, Chrissy opened the magazine she had packed in her flight bag. The gorgeous models in the fashion spreads didn't interest her. Even the delicious food pictures in the "Let's Party" section didn't catch her eye. Finally, she closed the magazine and leaned back against her seat.

It was time to face the truth. Sure, she'd told her parents she was excited about going to college. And she had joked with her brothers when they warned her not to get so brainy that she couldn't get a boyfriend. But now she had to face the fact that she was nervous. There were going to be thousands of students at the university.

Chrissy could only hope she'd be lucky enough to find the dining hall that night. How was she supposed to find her classes on such a huge campus? What if the courses were too difficult? She'd heard about all the work college professors gave their students.

I've got to calm down, she told herself. She'd wanted to go to Colorado University so much that it had hurt when she was placed on the waiting list. It would be silly to spoil her first day of college by being a worrywart.

She bet her cool, sophisticated cousin Caroline wasn't wringing her hands wondering whether or not she would find her way to the dining hall. Chrissy felt herself relax when she thought about the fact that Caroline would be starting as a freshman at Colorado University as well. Chrissy had applied to C.U. because Caroline had, and she was glad that things had worked out so they could go to college together. Otherwise, Chrissy had planned to attend Iowa State. Once she and Caroline had settled in their dorm room together, everything would be fine. Neither one of them would have to face the campus alone.

"Could I get you something, miss?" A flight attendant asked.

Startled out of her daydream, Chrissy noticed the cart and realized how dry her mouth was. "A Coke, please."

By the time she finished her drink, she felt much better. She and Caroline were going to meet new people and make lots of new friends. And she bet there would be hundreds of things to do around campus, things she couldn't even begin to imagine. Starting college was more exciting than her first day at Maxwell High in San Francisco, when she'd gone to live with Caroline, Aunt Edith, and Uncle Richard.

In fact, now that she thought about it, college might be easier. At Maxwell, she'd been the only new kid in the junior class. This time, all the freshmen would be new—and nervous. If she had to say so herself, she'd managed to fit in pretty well at Maxwell though she'd never attended a big-city high school before. After Maxwell High, Colorado University should be a piece of cake. Chrissy could barely remember why she'd been worried in the first place.

"What are you smiling about?" the man next to her asked when he tucked his briefcase under his seat.

"Am I smiling?"

"Oh, yes."

"I was just thinking about how much fun I'm going to have in college."

The man studied her for a moment and smiled. "From the twinkle in your eyes, I sure hope the folks in Boulder are ready for you."

"Is your tea too hot?"

Caroline Kirby looked up at her mother with surprise. "I don't think so."

"Well, you've only taken one sip."

"I guess I've been thinking," Caroline told her parents. She gazed beyond the coffee shop and suddenly noticed Denver's Stapleton Airport was a busy place. People were hurrying in all directions and it seemed as if arriving and outgoing flights were being announced every thirty seconds. But her jumbled thoughts were far more confusing than the minor distractions of the airport.

Her father raised his eyebrows. "You've been able to think with all this noise? I'll bet you're thinking about Luke."

"Not really, but I sure am looking forward to being in the same state with him finally."

Caroline hadn't planned to fall in love with one of her cousin's neighbors when she'd visited Chrissy and her family in Danbury, Iowa two years ago. But she and Luke hadn't been able to ignore their feelings for each other. There had been some rough times; living over a thousand miles apart didn't make romance easy. But at last, those days of having an impossibly long-distance relationship were over for them.

"I know you kept your relationship going during high school even though Luke was in Iowa and you were in California, but you'll both have so many new experiences in college," her mother said, sounding concerned.

"Sure Luke will be busy at the Air Force Academy in Fort Collins, but we're only going to be a few hours apart. We'll be able to see each other on weekends. After the fabulous time we had when I visited Chrissy a few weeks ago, I know things are going to work out for us!"

Mr. Kirby cleared his throat.

"Anyway, Dad, I was thinking about school," Caroline added.

"Excited?" her mother asked.

"Sort of." Caroline hesitated to share her fears, but finally concluded that her parents might have some good advice. Heaven knew she could use some helpful suggestions. "I just don't know what to expect from college or how well I'll handle things. What if my classes are too hard? What if I can't make friends?"

"You haven't had problems making friends in the past," her father said.

"But it wasn't easy," Caroline responded glumly. Her father was so busy with his career as a music critic that he probably hadn't noticed how long it had taken her to succeed socially at Maxwell High back home in San Francisco. Until she'd become part of a popular group in high school, she hadn't been very happy. "And now I won't even have you and Mom to cheer me up if things get rough."

Mrs. Kirby reached across the table and touched Caroline's hand. "I'm nervous, too, honey."

"*You're* nervous?" Caroline had seen her mother reschedule receptions for artists who came into town a day early or showed up a week late—owning an art gallery wasn't easy work. How could her mother be nervous about her going to college?

Her mother sniffed delicately. "My baby is leaving home."

"I'm hardly a baby," Caroline giggled.

"You know what I mean." Her mom blinked back tears. "You've been around the house for eighteen years. Now it's going to be just your dad and me. Things are changing for us, too."

"It's hard to believe you're going away to college," her father added. "You grew up so fast."

Caroline didn't think her eighteen years had passed so quickly. When she was small, it had taken absolutely forever for Christmas to come. And honestly, it had taken years for her to get a body that any guy would look at twice. Apparently, time was a matter of opinion.

"But don't worry about us," her mother said after she'd been the one who had said she would be lonely. "These are going to the best years of your life, Cara. Enjoy them."

"But, Mother, the decisions I make in college are going to have a major effect on the rest of my life!"

Her mother smiled sympathetically. "Don't be so dramatic. You won't have to make all those decisions your first day. In fact, you'll have four years to make most of them."

Why didn't her parents understand she had to meet the right people in college if she wanted to be successful in life? Also, she had to be sure to make the right impression on those people when she met them. With all that on her mind, how was she supposed to enjoy herself? She didn't consider asking for more advice since they probably would tell her to relax and have fun during the "best years of her life."

"You won't be completely on your own," her father reminded her. "Chrissy is going to be a freshman at Colorado University, also."

How could she forget her boisterous cousin when they were sitting in the coffee shop waiting for her plane to arrive? "I know Chrissy will be there."

"She will probably need your help adjusting," her mother said.

"Chrissy?" The girl who could walk into a disaster and come out a winner every time?

"I know she fit in with your friends at home." When her mother seemed to be reading her mind, Caroline took a sip of tea. "But college will be very different from Maxwell High."

Caroline choked on her cold tea. "You can say that again." Of course, college would be different. Why else did they think she was so worried?

"If you are this worried," said Mrs. Kirby, "imagine how Chrissy must be feeling right now."

Although her cousin had made it look easy, Caroline knew how hard it had been for Chrissy to settle in to a new school and fit in with a new crowd. The big city had been such a change from the Madden farm in Danbury, Iowa. Chrissy had missed her parents and her brothers. She probably wasn't looking forward to starting all over again any more than Cara was.

Her mother tried once more to make her point. "She's probably feeling a lot of stress."

"If Chrissy's nervous, we'll all hear about it," Caroline said, knowing her cousin never kept anything to herself. Chrissy didn't seem to understand that sometimes it was smarter not to blurt out the truth. What upperclassman was going to think it was cute when Chrissy got lost and admitted to the world the campus was almost as big as the entire town of Danbury, Iowa? "I guess she might need some help."

"It would be nice if you made a point of being supportive for the first few days," Caroline's mother suggested.

"Cara! Aunt Edith! Uncle Richard!"

Caroline shrank back against her chair when she heard Chrissy shrieking their names across the airport. She couldn't see her cousin yet, but she would recognize that voice anywhere.

Her father pushed back his chair and stood up to get a better view of the room. "You have to admit that girl has a lot of spirit."

"That's one way to describe her," Caroline's mother said as she joined her husband.

Caroline was the last one to move away from the table. With a sigh, she counted herself lucky. It was a good thing she hadn't made any promises about sticking to her cousin's side. She knew exactly what kind of impression she'd make on the people she was dying to meet if she had to be Chrissy's body guard.

She stood in time to see Chrissy cutting through the crowd to get to the coffee shop, hitting people with her purse and two overstuffed bags as she moved toward them. She almost slapped a man in the face when she waved at them exuberantly. Caroline knew it had been silly for any of them to worry about Chrissy. She looked more excited than a five-year-old kid on Christmas Eve. Apparently, she didn't know enough to get nervous about what lay ahead for them.

Chrissy stopped in front of Caroline's parents and let go of her bags. One dropped on her father's foot before he could jump out of the way.

"Sorry, Uncle Richard. I just wanted both hands free so I could hug you!"

Everyone in the coffee shop was staring at them. Caroline knew this kind of thing happened everywhere Chrissy went, but in the back of her mind she had thought things might be different now that they were both older. It had been silly for her to think Chrissy would change just because she was going to college.

Chrissy climbed over one of her bags to grab both of her cousin's hands. "Cara, isn't this great! We're college women!"

"It's super," she managed to say without any of Chrissy's enthusiasm. Chrissy was acting like they were on their way to an amusement park, instead of starting the most important part of their lives!

"We have to get my luggage. I have tons of it. My mom even bought me a new trunk!" she told Caroline's father. "How are we going to fit it all in the taxi?"

"We've arranged for someone to deliver all of your and Cara's luggage to the campus," he explained.

"That's smart! Remember my first time in the airport when I came to San Francisco?" Chrissy asked, turning back to her cousin. "I wanted to ride on the luggage carousel!" She threw back her head and laughed.

"Don't remind me," Caroline muttered. Maybe she'd been wrong to think Chrissy couldn't change. She seemed to realize now how silly she'd been two years ago. There was hope—at least a slim hope—that Chrissy could be a regular college student just like everyone else.

Chapter 2

"Are you sure we can't be together?" Chrissy leaned across the desk toward the woman in charge of room assignments.

The woman shook her head in a no-nonsense manner. "I'm sorry, Ms. Madden. While you were on the waiting list, your cousin was assigned a room and a roommate."

"Couldn't we at least be in the same dorm?" she asked, wondering why all the questions had to come from her. Caroline was being awfully quiet behind her.

"No," said the woman with a definitive shake of her head.

Chrissy frowned. "Why not?"

"Because everything has been arranged. You

are in Culver Hall, and Ms. Kirby has a room in Fielding Hall."

Uncle Richard rested a hand on her shoulder. "Let's go find your rooms. I just saw a van arrive from the airport. Maybe it's the one with your packages."

It was a short walk to the dormitories, still, by the time they got to Chrissy's room, the driver had most of her things unloaded. "Where did you put my stuff?" she demanded.

"In your room."

"I don't have a room," she said in an irritated tone. As if it wasn't bad enough to be living away from Caroline, now she was going to have to track down where he'd left her things in this huge dormitory.

"Room four-fifty," he told her. "The lady at the front desk will give you your keys."

Caroline's family waited while Chrissy collected her keys and a list of dorm rules. "Want to see my room?" she asked, gesturing for them to accompany her.

Chrissy watched Caroline look up at her father. Cara was probably anxious to see her own room, but she wasn't ready to be left alone yet. With her own family back in Iowa, the Kirbys were the only people she knew at Colorado University. Why couldn't Cara share them for a just a little while?

Aunt Edith must have read her mind. "Sure, we'll walk you up to your room," she said. "I'd like to see where you'll be living."

"Great! Follow me." They found an elevator and rode up to the fourth floor. Chrissy tapped the key against her open palm and hummed along with the rock music they heard coming from various rooms.

"How will you girls ever get any studying done with all this noise?" Uncle Richard asked.

"They're all just excited about moving in," Aunt Edith assured him. "I can tell you never lived in a girls' dorm!"

Chrissy smiled as they teased each other, but her grin faded when they arrived at room four-fifty.

"Hi! I'm Denise Crawley," a short, brown-haired girl called out. "Is one of you Christine Madden?"

"I'm Chrissy." She stepped forward and swallowed hard. This was the person she was going to be living with instead of Caroline. Inside the room, the two beds were heaped with suitcases. The floor was so littered with trunks and bags that it would be impossible to get near the two desks.

Aunt Edith squeezed her hand. "It's cute. You're going to love it here."

Chrissy stared at her aunt, convinced that she had to be kidding. Although she and Cara had been a little cramped sharing the upstairs bedroom in the Kirbys' San Francisco apartment, that room had been spacious in comparison with the tiny crowded room she saw before her. It was a miracle that two beds, two desks, and two dressers could even fit!

"I can't wait to see my room!" Caroline said with a grin.

Chrissy wondered why her cousin was so excited. Was she imagining all kinds of great things she could do to decorate her room, or was she expecting to find a larger room in Fielding Hall?

Uncle Richard cleared his throat. "We do need to get going. Will you be all right, Chrissy?"

Chrissy was surprised by the burning feeling in her throat. What in the world did she have to cry about? A few months ago, going to a college like Colorado University had been a wild daydream—she should be thrilled by the opportunities that were ahead!

"I'll be fine," she whispered. It seemed like it took only seconds for her aunt and uncle to hug her and for Caroline to mumble something about seeing her later. When they left, she turned and tried to hide her tears from her new roommate.

"It's hard being on your own," Denise told her. "Being busy helps."

Chrissy sniffed. "How do you know?" She had assumed her roommate was another freshman, but she sounded pretty experienced.

"My parents left an hour ago." With a silly grin, she admitted, "I sat on my bed and cried for fifteen minutes and then I decided it would be more productive to start unpacking."

It seemed like a reasonable idea. Chrissy

opened one of the suitcases on her bed. "Which dresser and closet are mine?"

"I took these." Denise pointed to the furniture closest to the bed holding her almost-empty suitcases. "I didn't know . . . I mean, since I was here first . . .

"It's okay," Chrissy told her roommate quickly, deciding that, after all, Denise might be just as nervous as she was.

"Where are you from?" Denise asked, carrying a heavy winter jacket to the closet.

"Iowa."

"Really?" Denise said enthusiastically. "I'm from a little town outside Omaha."

"But I've lived with my cousin in San Francisco for the last two years." Chrissy sucked on her lower lip. Maybe Denise thought it was great they were roommates, but Chrissy Madden hadn't come all the way to a college in Colorado just to live with a farm kid.

Before the acceptance letter arrived from Colorado University, she had been ready to go to Iowa State. If she'd wanted to hang out with farm kids from the Midwest, she would be moving into a dorm in Ames, Iowa right now instead of being here in Culver Hall.

"California must have been . . . interesting," Denise said quietly.

Chrissy felt her cheeks heat up when she realized how snobbish she must have sounded. *Who am I to knock farmers?* she thought. Growing up, she'd been a farm kid like all of her friends. But

after two years on the coast, she'd come home to
Iowa and found that she missed living in a big
city. It occurred to her that she might not be the
only midwestern girl who wasn't a hick. She had
to give Denise a chance.

"Do you have any ideas for fixing up our
room?" she asked, completely changing the sub-
ject.

"The RA, I mean the resident assistant, said we
could bunk our beds if we want more space,"
Denise said, still sounding cautious after Chrissy's
abrupt remark.

"Can I have the top one?" Chrissy asked with a
grin. "I've always wanted to sleep in a top bunk."

Denise laughed. "No problem. I've had the top
bunk ever since I started sharing a room with my
little sister."

"You have a sister? I just have a pack of brothers. That's why I like my cousin Caroline so
much. You know, the other girl who was with
me?"

"Your cousin must be very different from my
little sister. She constantly borrows my clothes
and never gives them back until she has spilled
something on them." She held up a white sweater
which had apparently escaped her little sister's
notice. "Don't get me wrong. I love the little brat,
but I'm so excited to have new clothes that she
can't ruin!"

"I'm afraid my cousin Caroline got very tired of
my borrowing her clothes—but I promise I won't
lay a hand on yours!" Chrissy joked. Chrissy

sighed and relaxed for the first time since the woman who assigned rooms said she couldn't live with Caroline. Denise was going to be all right. She could relate to someone who loved her family in spite of the fact that they made her crazy.

"What can we do about the walls?" Denise pointed out the stained plaster near her bed.

"Hang posters," Chrissy suggested after a moment.

"Of men?" asked Denise excitedly.

"Why not?" said Chrissy.

"We're going to get along great!" Denise exclaimed.

"I think so, too!" agreed Chrissy.

It took over two hours for them to find a man who would put their single beds together to make a bunk bed. Chrissy climbed up to her perch and hung her feet over the edge. "So do you want to go shopping for posters after orientation tomorrow?"

"Yes. And we need to find an extension cord," Denise reminded her. They had decided to put Denise's sound system on the window ledge, but the cord was too short to reach any of the outlets.

"What do you think they'll do to us at orientation?" Chrissy wondered aloud.

"Tell us all the rules," Denise answered.

"And we have to pick our classes. What are you taking?" Chrissy asked. She couldn't imagine how anyone could make a decision with so many choices.

"I know I have to take a language because I never took one in high school," said Denise.

"I'm going to sign up for French," Chrissy told her. "My cousin knows it, and I'm hoping she can help me. Why don't you take it, too?"

"Good idea. What about science?"

"I thought all the freshman had to take biology," said Chrissy.

"Will we have to cut things up?" Denise made a gagging sound, but Chrissy couldn't see her in the lower bunk.

"I suppose. Try not to get placed in the section that meets right after lunch," Chrissy advised.

"Are you going to join any clubs?" Denise asked.

"I hope so. I think that's the best way to meet people," Chrissy said. From the phone conversations she'd had with her cousin during the last few weeks, it seemed to Chrissy that Caroline was almost too serious about meeting people, instead of using the clubs on campus as a way to have fun.

"But what if the classes are hard? I'm worried I won't have time for clubs *and* homework."

Chrissy smiled as she lay in her upper bunk. It was nice to know she wasn't the only one worrying about how hard the classes were going to be. "I guess we'll just have to wait and find out. But I want to join at least one club during my first semester."

"Four o'clock. Dinner starts in an hour!" some-one cried in the hallway.

"That's Kristine, our RA," Denise explained.

"Four o'clock!" Chrissy jumped down from the top bunk. "We've been talking for three hours! I bet my cousin has been waiting for me to visit her."

"Will you be back for dinner?"

Chrissy looked back at her roommate and real-ized that Denise didn't have a cousin on campus. Denise probably didn't know anyone else who would eat dinner with her.

"Sure," Chrissy promised. "I'll see you a little later."

Fielding Hall was just across the lawn from Culver, so Chrissy found the ivy-covered dorm quickly. The girl at the reception desk directed her to room 136.

"Who is it?" a strange voice asked when she knocked.

"Chrissy Madden." She heard her cousin talk-ing to someone in the room, and then Caroline opened the door.

"Hi, Chrissy."

"Hi." She waited for her cousin to back up and let her into the room, wondering why she was acting so strangely. "May I come in?"

"Sure." Caroline stepped back and Chrissy saw a girl with short, dark hair sitting on a bed cov-ered with a light blue satin quilt.

When she stepped inside the room, Chrissy discovered that both beds had the same blue covers and their window was hung with matching drapes. "Boy, your room sure looks different from mine!"

"Thanks to my roommate, Ellis Lattimore," said Caroline. "She arrived yesterday. Luckily, she had time to pick up the linens in Denver this morning after she checked out the room."

Linens? When had her cousin started calling bedspreads *linens*? And who had a name like Ellis? Chrissy narrowed her eyes and took a good look at Caroline's roommate. Her short hair was cut in the same style they had seen all over New York. Her Colorado University T-shirt hung loosely over what appeared to be a very thin body. In fact, Chrissy wondered how her neck was strong enough to support her heavy gold necklace.

"Who's your friend?" Ellis asked. Chrissy felt as if her full floral shirt had been diagnosed as sinfully unstylish.

"My . . . cousin, Chrissy Madden."

"She's related to you?"

"She's from Iowa," Caroline explained.

Chrissy didn't think her cousin needed to make "Iowa" sound like an excuse for her clothing. She had simply chosen something comfortable for the airplane.

"Where are you from? New York?" Chrissy asked Ellis, trying not to sound as defensive as she felt.

She giggled in a way that sounded like hiccups

to Chrissy, but she supposed Ellis thought it was cute since she didn't make any effort to stop.

"Me? New York? Why no. I'm from Denver," Ellis laughed.

"Then you must know a lot about the university," Chrissy said, making herself comfortable on Caroline's bed. If Ellis was from Denver, then she couldn't be as sophisticated as she was pretending to be, Chrissy decided. But maybe Ellis could offer some good advice about the campus.

"I guess I know a few things," Ellis said flippantly.

"My roommate, Denise, and I were talking about classes. What do you know about registration?" Chrissy asked.

"Classes?"

Chrissy shook her head, certain her hearing had gone bad. The girl sounded as though choosing classes was the last thing on her list of priorities.

"I guess you don't have any clues about what are the best classes," she concluded before turning to her cousin. "Cara, I told Denise that you'd be happy to help us both with our French assignments."

"*Le français*?" Ellis interrupted.

Caroline looked over at Ellis before she said, "Well, I don't know how much time I'll have to help you."

"Oh." It seemed to Chrissy like Caroline was trying to impress her roommate, but that would be silly. Her cousin was a super person, and Ellis

Lattimore seemed like she was going to turn out to be a big phony. "Denise and I were just talking about all the campus activities we can get involved in."

"Really?" Ellis held her breath as though waiting for Chrissy to say something to make her laugh.

Chrissy had seen people like her before in California. She wasn't afraid of Ellis. "Sure. I figure tomorrow we'll find out about all the rules, clubs, and classes. I can't wait!"

Ellis covered her mouth with a delicate hand, showing off her long red nails. Somehow, she didn't quite manage to hide her smile. "Oh, Cara. It's so hard to believe that the two of you are related!"

Chrissy stared at Ellis in disbelief. It wasn't so much Ellis's rude remark, but her casual use of Caroline's nickname that bothered Chrissy. She'd try for her cousin's sake, but Chrissy wasn't sure if she and Ellis would ever be friends!

Chapter 3

"Rise and shine!"

Ellis peeked out of the bathroom Thursday morning, her mascara wand poised over her right eye. "What's going on?"

Caroline ran a hand though her hair. "I hate to admit it, but it sounds like my cousin."

"The country mouse?" Ellis giggled.

Caroline didn't answer. She didn't like the way Ellis had treated Chrissy yesterday afternoon, but she couldn't very well tell her roommate to knock it off. Considering the way Ellis had decorated the room, and the way she'd talked about her campus connections after Chrissy left, Caroline couldn't afford to offend her new roommate.

There was a sharp knock on the door. "Cara? Are you in there?"

Caroline hurried to open the door before Ellis could say anything else. "Good morning, Chrissy."

"Hi." Her cousin strode into the room with a small brunette tagging behind her.

"You remember Denise, my roommate," Chrissy said as though she should have immediately recognized the girl she'd only seen for a moment yesterday in Culver Hall.

"Nice to meet you, Denise," she said politely. "I'm Chrissy's cousin, Caroline."

"I know. She's told me all about you."

Denise seemed very friendly. Dressed in jeans and a pink sweat shirt, she looked like a perfect roommate for Chrissy. Caroline couldn't help thinking that it was a good thing that they'd been assigned to different dorms. Ellis would be able to introduce her to the right people, and Chrissy would probably get along just fine with Denise.

"We thought you might like to walk with us to Fillmore Auditorium," Chrissy said, finally explaining the reason for the visit.

"I was going to go with Ellis."

"Really? I wasn't sure Ellis would be going." Chrissy leaned closer to her cousin. "You know, she didn't seem too impressed with the idea of registering for classes."

"Of course she's going to orientation. We're all freshmen."

"*Shh* . . . People don't have to know we're

freshmen if we're careful." Ellis came out of the bathroom looking absolutely glamorous. Caroline promised herself she'd ask for advice on eye makeup sometime when Chrissy wasn't hanging around.

"I'm not ashamed," Chrissy declared, standing tall. "There is so much to learn around here. It's going to be fun. Why pretend you're an experienced upperclassman if you're not."

"We should be going if we don't want to miss any of our orientation," Denise reminded Chrissy.

"Everyone ready?" Chrissy asked, her gaze settling on Ellis.

Ellis touched her ears to make sure her clunky earrings were in place. "Let's hit Fillmore."

Chrissy took a deep breath of fresh air when they got outside. "Isn't it great here?" She gestured expansively. "The sky is so blue. The sun is shining on the yellow aspens and the orange maple trees—it's all so wonderful!"

Next to Caroline, Ellis rolled her eyes, and Caroline had to agree silently with her roommate. Sure, it was their first official day as college students, but that meant it was time to act like an adult. Chrissy was more excited than a kid at her own birthday party. Wouldn't she ever grow up?

"Look at all those students!" Chrissy exclaimed, suddenly stopping at the bottom of the steps in front of the auditorium.

Ellis had been checking her nails and stumbled into both Chrissy and Denise. Caroline stared at the sidewalk, determined not to laugh.

"What's the delay?" Ellis inquired. "Why are you two just standing there?"

"I just had to stop and save this picture in my mind. Isn't it neat the way the mountains rise up behind the building? I'll want to remember this day when I'm fifty."

"*Pleeease* . . . ," Ellis begged. "Don't even mention it—I'm never going to be old."

"Let's sit up front so we don't miss anything," said Chrissy as she raced ahead.

Caroline and Ellis followed the other girls as they found seats in the third row of the auditorium. Minutes after they sat down, a man came to the podium and tapped the microphone twice.

"Hello and welcome to Colorado University. I am Ken James, the dean of student affairs . . ."

The rather young man went on to explain campus rules such as no alcoholic beverages in the dormitories and the probation policies regarding unsatisfactory grades. In the middle of it all, Ellis poked Caroline in the ribs.

"Your cousin's a hoot. Look at her—she's taking notes!"

Caroline had to bite her lower lip hard to keep from dying of embarrassment. Chrissy was not only listening intently, she was scribbling notes. She wished she could tell her cousin to relax. There wasn't going to be a test at the end of this particular lecture.

They were told to consult the packets they had been sent in the mail during the last two weeks.

Chrissy and Denise had their counselor assignments with them; the other girls did not.

"We'll walk back to Fielding Hall with you while you get your forms," Chrissy offered.

"Thanks, but it's not necessary," Ellis hurriedly replied.

"No problem. Neither of us have our counselor appointments until after eleven o'clock." When Chrissy tried to make eye contact, Caroline glanced in the other direction. "If we break up now, we won't be able to go through registration together."

"Cara?" Ellis asked her roommate. "Were you worried about getting through registration on your own?"

Actually, Caroline thought it would be nice to have someone to talk with while she waited for her turn, but she didn't want Ellis to laugh at her or think she was a loser.

"Since I'm not sure what I'll be taking, I probably should do it alone," Caroline said carefully. "It might take me a while to figure out a schedule."

"Me, too. I might need your advice. We could hang out together," Chrissy insisted. Caroline had to wonder what it was going to take for her cousin to get the message.

"I'm sure I'll run into you later on." Caroline winced when Chrissy's smile flickered. She didn't want to hurt her cousin's feelings, but they had to start doing things on their own.

She knew that if Chrissy could have things her way, they would be taking all the same classes and living together. She could only thank the dean of student affairs, or whoever had decided to put them in separate dorms. The last thing they needed now was identical schedules.

Chrissy cleared her throat. "Well, Denise, would you like to walk over to the Administration Building with me?"

"Sure. In fact, let's stop at The Rocky Mountain Club."

"What's that?" Chrissy asked.

"It's the restaurant in the basement of the Student Union. I'll treat you to a morning Coke," Denise said sympathetically.

Caroline winced again as her cousin slowly walked away with Denise. Even the girl from Omaha had been able to tell that sweet, lovable Chrissy was being dumped on by her cousin.

"Don't worry about it." Ellis tapped her on the shoulder. "They're going to be fine together. She doesn't need you to be her baby-sitter."

She wanted to tell Ellis that it wasn't that way between them. Although she had shown Chrissy a lot about living in the big city when Chrissy had come to live with the Kirbys in San Francisco, Chrissy had taught her about opening up and trusting people. But Chrissy wasn't dumb. Caroline was sure her cousin would understand this was all a part of growing up and adjusting to college.

"We'll be here forever," the girl in front of Chrissy complained.

"I think we're going to miss our first classes before we ever get registered for them!" the boy behind her worried.

"There are more people in this line than in all of Danbury, Iowa!" Chrissy declared. She had seen crowds in San Francisco, but never this many people, all on line for the same thing.

"Iowa?" the boy asked.

"Sure, it's east of Nebraska and north of Missouri. Have you heard of it?" she teased him.

"Of course, I've heard of Iowa. But I never met anyone from there before."

"Where are you from?" she asked him.

"Oregon."

"I'm from Lincoln, Nebraska," the other girl volunteered.

"My roommate is from Omaha," Chrissy told her, and suddenly the line didn't seem so long and impersonal. She had already met two people. Maybe it would be all right that Cara hadn't wanted to come with her and that Denise was still waiting for her counselor appointment.

Chrissy understood that Caroline was really concerned about fitting in at college but Caroline's relationship with Ellis really puzzled her. Couldn't Caroline see that her roommate wasn't being a good friend to her? Friends didn't make fun of your family.

The girl in front of Chrissy stepped up to the registration window, and she tried to listen in on the conversation. But the guy behind her started talking. "Almost our turn. What are you taking?"

"Biology, political science—"

"I don't think it's fair that we can only take four classes," he interrupted.

"I think four will be plenty for me. They don't want anyone overloading themselves their first semester." Chrissy thought the dean of student affairs had made that point perfectly clear during his orientation speech.

The boy next to her shrugged as though the rule shouldn't apply to him. "I could handle five classes," he boasted.

The girl in front of Chrissy turned away from the window and groaned. "You're lucky if you can get half your classes. Two of my four first-choice classes were full already. Now I've got to take Anthropology one-oh-one at eight o'clock in the morning!"

"May I help you?" The woman behind the window sounded tired.

"Yes." Chrissy hated to miss hearing the rest of the girl's story, but it was her turn. She shoved her class list across the counter.

"American literature." The woman punched some numbers into a computer and nodded. "There's an opening."

She also had good news on Chrissy's other classes: political science, Biology 101, and French 101. Chrissy sighed with relief.

The woman printed out the class list in duplicate and set it on the counter for Chrissy's signature. Happy to be done with the long registration process, she signed it quickly and took her copy.

Though Caroline had refused to accompany her to registration, she'd completed it without a hitch. She was halfway to the door when she realized her class schedule did not include the introductory course Biology 101, but Biology 1001—Biogenetics and Ethics.

"Excuse me." She leaned against the counter, interrupting the boy who was currently talking to the woman. "There's a mistake in my schedule."

"Miss, it's not your turn," the woman said.

Chrissy stuck her face in front of the woman. "You just helped me with my schedule three minutes ago."

"I guess I did. What's the problem?"

Chrissy heard the boy sigh, but she ignored him. It would just take a minute for the woman to correct the mistake. "Look at my schedule. I asked for Biology one-oh-one, but you put me in an advanced class. I can't take it—I'm just a freshman!"

"You're right. A freshman can't take a one-thousand-level class."

"Then please fix it for me." Chrissy smiled.

"No."

"But you said I can't take the advanced class . . ." Chrissy said, a note of hysteria creeping into her voice.

"You'll have to transfer out of it."

"How?" There was probably some other line she had to stand in with a million other students. If that was the case, she wanted to get it over with as quickly as possible.

"You have to go to the class the first day it meets and get your card from the teacher. You drop that class and add the introductory class to your schedule—if there are still some openings in it."

Chrissy pressed a damp palm to her forehead. *This is turning into a big nightmare*, she thought. "You mean my biology class might be full by then?"

"Unfortunately, it could work out that way," the woman explained.

"Then why can't you add the right biology class to my schedule now?"

"The computer would spit out a card with five classes on it."

"So take the one-thousand class off my schedule and add the right one."

The woman shook her head. "My terminal has already sent your class schedule into the main computer. I can't change it from here."

"Do I really have to go to that class the first day?" Chrissy asked frantically. What if everyone thought she was such a stupid freshman that she'd asked for the advanced class on purpose?

The boy next to Chrissy cleared his throat, and she knew she'd have to give up for now. "Sorry," she mumbled as she walked away from the desk dejectedly.

Biology 1001? What did they do in that class— build their own Frankenstein monsters and bring them to life? Or maybe they did that gene-splitting stuff she'd read about in a science magazine. The man on the plane said his nephew hadn't planned to be a rocket scientist until he attended C.U. He'd probably asked for Engineering 101 and gotten stuck in an advanced engineering class instead! Although things had worked out all right for him, she could just see herself as the first kid on campus to hatch a two-headed chicken for her year-end project.

If only Caroline hadn't insisted on spending so much time with her new roommate, she'd be here right now to help me handle this awful situation! Chrissy thought. *What in the world am I going to do?*

Chapter 4

Chrissy hesitated for a moment before she knocked on Caroline's door. Why did she feel silly turning to her cousin when she was a little homesick? Denise was going to be a great roommate, but she had gone to meet some upperclassmen she knew from Omaha. The room seemed empty, even with the hunk posters they'd hung on the walls.

Things looked brighter when she realized Ellis might not be home. She knocked.

Caroline opened the door and smiled. "Hi, Chrissy. Come on in."

Thinking her cousin sounded more friendly than she had either yesterday or earlier that morning, Chrissy figured Ellis was gone. But the little princess was sitting in the middle of her blue satin quilt, reading a magazine. Determined to be polite, Chrissy said, "Hi, Ellis."

Ellis nodded once. Chrissy assumed that was her way of acknowledging people she didn't really want to see, but she wasn't going to let her cousin's roommate get her down.

"Are you registered?" Chrissy asked her cousin.

Caroline sat on the edge of her bed and motioned for Chrissy to join her. "Yes. I'm taking art history, European history before 1600, French literature, and Introduction to Biology."

"I'm taking biology, too." Chrissy couldn't help thinking how great it would be if they were in the same section. "At least, I hope I'll be taking the introductory class."

"What?" Caroline raised her eyebrows as if expecting to find out Chrissy had done something incredibly strange. "Didn't you register for Biology one-oh-one?"

"Sure. But they put me in Biology one thousand-one instead of one hundred-one."

"Are you a science brain or something?" Ellis asked, looking up in surprise. "I thought only a senior could take a one-oh-oh-one class. What is it about?"

"Bio-something and ethics," Chrissy explained.

"You're not sure what the class is about, but you signed up for it anyway?" Caroline shook her head in dismay.

Chrissy had to laugh—her cousin thought the very worst of her. She might have been that naive when she came to California two years ago, but she knew a lot more about the world now. "I didn't sign up for it, the lady at registration punched the wrong numbers into her computer."

"Why didn't you ask her to fix it?" Caroline said in a more sympathetic tone.

"I did ask, but once the information is in the main computer, it can't be changed until the first day of classes."

"That's ridiculous." Ellis declared. "Are you sure you've got the story right?"

"Rules are rules around here," Chrissy told the girls, who apparently hadn't learned much about the bureaucracy yet. Trying to hide how nervous she was about changing her schedule, she said "But that isn't the worst thing that happened to me today. I bought my books—they cost over a hundred dollars!"

"My art-history book alone cost forty-five," Caroline said without a hint of the shock that Chrissy had felt in the campus bookstore.

"I wanted to shop around, but there's no other place to buy the books we need for our classes." It almost seemed illegal to Chrissy. "Shouldn't there be a discount store?"

Ellis surprised Chrissy by snorting loudly. "There's always used books, if you don't mind books that have been written in. Didn't you see them stacked at the back of the store?"

"I checked," Chrissy said. "None of the books that I needed were in the used stack."

"Well, it seems like you've learned a lot about

campus life the hard way. How do you like it?" Caroline asked.

"I love it." Chrissy pulled a folded piece of paper out of the back pocket of her non-designer jeans. "Have you seen this?"

Caroline tried to squint at the sheet. "What is it?"

"A list of the all the clubs having meetings next week. I can't believe how many organizations a person could join. There's the International Students Association, the Women Students Consortium, a million sororities and fraternities, a crisis line—"

"We get the idea," Ellis interrupted.

"What do you suppose the International Students Association does? I might like to have a penpal," Chrissy said thoughtfully.

Ellis laughed out loud. The sound reminded Chrissy of a braying donkey. "The International Students Association is where all the foreign students meet to talk about culture shock."

"Sounds like a good idea," Chrissy mumbled. She could imagine how it could shock someone from another country to run into Ellis.

"Are either of you interested in the Women Students Consortium?"she asked.

"I don't think so," Caroline said.

"Why not? Wouldn't it be nice to get together with a bunch of girls and talk about things?"

"We can do that in the dorm. The consortium is probably some feminist group," Caroline guessed.

"Really," Ellis added. "Not that I don't want equality and all, but I have better ways to spend my days than standing in a picket line with a bunch of girls who can't get dates."

"They probably wouldn't want you, anyway," Chrissy couldn't help telling Ellis.

"You're right," she said. "It wouldn't be right to join a group like that unless you truly supported all their causes."

Chrissy smiled to herself. Ellis had completely missed the point. If the women held some kind of rally they would probably welcome everyone to participate—everyone except Ellis—who would give their demonstration a bad name. She'd probably drop her picket sign the minute she broke a nail.

"So what groups are you going to join if it's not the International Students Association or the Women's Consortium?" Chrissy asked Ellis and Caroline.

"I want to check around and see what kind of reputation the different groups have," Caroline said.

Ellis nodded. "That's a smart move. You want to be sure you're with the right people."

"But how do you know they're the right people until you get to know them?" Chrissy asked. "Besides, I thought you joined a club to make new friends and have fun."

"I wish it were that simple." Caroline frowned.

"It can be. Just pick a club that sounds fun, and

go to their first meeting. That's what I'm going to do."

Ellis tapped her chin with a long red fingernail. "Now why did I just know you were going to say that?"

"Do you really want to go this dorm party?" Ellis asked as she and Caroline were dressing.

"I think we have to go. But do you believe the Fielding Hall upperclassmen are going to give up their first Friday night on campus to party with the freshmen?"

Ellis shrugged. "Everyone says it's a tradition."

"I know. Chrissy is jealous that her dorm doesn't have any traditions."

"That sounds like something your cousin would say. Has she joined the campus Optimists Club yet?" Ellis was trying to choose between pearl earrings in one hand and a bright blue enameled pair in the other.

"I like the blue ones for a dorm party," Caroline told her, deciding not to respond to Ellis's comment about Chrissy.

"I don't want to be a hostess tonight,"Ellis complained.

"Really," Caroline agreed. "I don't know how we're supposed to throw a welcome-home party for upperclassmen who we've never met. Do you believe that some alumni agreed to fund the dorm renovation only if the freshmen continued to hold this party every year?"

Ellis laughed softly. "I'm sure the college

administration was willing to agree to anything to get the bucks."

"Ladies, ladies," someone called in the hall. "It's nearly time."

Connie, the resident assistant, peeked into Caroline's room and said, "That includes you, too, Ellis."

Caroline ran a brush through her hair for a second and then wondered why she was worried about how she looked. No one was going to see her except a bunch of girls in the dorm living room.

Ellis slipped her small feet into black flats. "At least we managed to avoid making those dumb sandwiches."

Caroline giggled. "Shopping was much more fun than cutting bread into triangles. I loved that boutique we found."

"I vote we make our appearance and then sneak back upstairs," Ellis whispered as they joined the other girls in the hall.

Caroline was stunned when she saw the large living room crowded with women. Most of them weren't just freshmen she hadn't seen around the dorm. Most of these people were older, and several were very pretty and sophisticated. It was hard to believe they had come to this party to talk to freshmen.

Connie handed sandwich trays to both Caroline and Ellis with directions that they should mingle and feed the guests. Caroline had to laugh at Ellis's cross-eyed expression when she realized she was expected to serve the upperclassmen.

"Have you seen Roger?" one girl asked a redhead who was reaching for one of Caroline's sandwiches.

"Roger?" The redhead rolled her eyes. "He met some lifeguard with a body that could make a guy crazy, or so he says."

"You mean it's over between you?"

"Yeah." She looked at Caroline and smiled. "Do you have a boyfriend?"

"I'm seeing someone at the Air Force Academy." She had to smile when she thought of how well things had turned out for her and Luke.

"Good luck," the first girl advised.

"We plan to visit each other a lot," she told them, sure they didn't understand her situation.

The redhead reached for a punch glass from another passing tray. "We're not trying to be mean or anything, but not many high-school relationships survive freshman year."

"Don't look so worried," the other girl said. "There are so many guys here at C.U. that you won't have time to wonder what your boyfriend is doing in his spare time at the Academy."

Someone grabbed Cara's elbow. "You've got to come over here."

Ellis nearly dragged her to the crowd of girls sitting on loveseats in the corner. People were perched on the arms and kneeling on the floor listening to four juniors discuss life at C.U.

". . . so I told Professor Taylor he could forget it. I wasn't going to write a paper on the Miss

America Pageant. After all, my sister was the
vice-president of the Women Students
Consortium. She would have gotten me kicked
out of my family!"

"She was in his sociology class," Ellis whispered
as she slid Caroline's sandwich tray under an end
table. "He's supposed to be one of the craziest
teachers on campus."

"What did Taylor do?" someone asked.

"He said that was fine, I could still get my B plus
if I researched the Mr. Universe contest."

"Did you do it?" Caroline found herself asking,
but no one seemed to hear her. She wondered if
she would have the nerve to refuse an assignment that seemed stupid.

"Are you a sociology major?" the girl next to
Ellis asked.

The older girl laughed. "Me? I want to be an
elementary-school teacher. But I had to have
twelve social-science credits and sociology
sounded easy—until I took the class."

The older girls talked about classes, teachers,
parties, and men until the party broke up after
midnight. Caroline could barely straighten her
knees when she finally tried to get up off the
floor.

"And we were going to sneak out early," Ellis
whispered on their way back to their room.

"You know what? I really feel like a college
woman after listening to those upperclassmen
talk," Caroline confided.

"And we haven't been to a single class yet."

Ellis smiled. "Didn't you like the way the older girls made it sound like every time you turn around on this campus you can meet a great guy?"

Caroline slipped her key into their lock. "I haven't met any yet."

"You're not supposed to," Ellis reminded her. "You've already got a boyfriend in Fort Collins. The rest of us should have first pick when it comes to the guys on campus."

Thinking about Luke, Caroline sat down and told herself the older girls weren't necessarily right. They didn't understand how unique and special their relationship was. There might be hundreds of unattached, gorgeous guys on campus, but Caroline Kirby wasn't even going to be tempted. Why change a single thing about her life? She had Luke, a great roommate who understood her, and she was a college woman at last!

Chapter 5

"Are you sure you want to do this?" Ellis asked Caroline Sunday afternoon.

"Yes. Joining Sigma Theda will be a great way to get involved on campus." Caroline checked her reflection in the mirror for the fourth time. "Do I look all right?"

Ellis frowned as she studied Caroline. "The silk dress is perfect for the Sigmas, but you need pearls."

"I don't have any," she answered despondently. Caroline thought longingly about how she had often borrowed pearls from her mother when she lived at home during high school.

"Don't worry," Ellis reassured her. "You can wear mine."

"Are you sure? I mean, you don't seem too hot

about Sigma Theda." Caroline peered over her shoulder, checking her panty hose for any runs down the back of her legs. The Sigma Thedas were known for noticing little details.

"Hey, just because I don't want to join a sorority myself, doesn't mean it wouldn't be a great move for you. I'll admit the Sigmas are the most socially prominent group on campus. You'll definitely meet some interesting people—and it wouldn't hurt your social life, either, in case you and Luke break up."

Caroline laughed. She and Luke *were not* going to break up, but it was great to have a roommate who considered all the possibilities. When she'd called Chrissy for the meeting place and time, Caroline had been frustrated by Chrissy's questions about why she wanted to join some Greek club. Throughout the entire phone call with her cousin, she wished she hadn't tried to impress Ellis by throwing away her own freshman orientation roster of "silly" campus meetings. Then she could have avoided that irritating conversation with Chrissy.

Ellis fastened the pearls around Caroline's neck. "You look great. They're going to love you!"

"I hope so." Caroline made a big deal of crossing her fingers, and Ellis laughed.

She still had her fingers crossed when she reached the three-block area on Aspen Street where the sorority and fraternity houses dominated both sides of the road. Some sorority at 140

Aspen was having a party as well. The girls talking on the porch were very well dressed. In case
the Sigma Thedas didn't fall in love with her, this
sorority might be a good second choice.

It seemed odd to Caroline that the prestigious
Sigma Theda sorority would have their house at
the end of Greek territory. When she found 124
Aspen, she carefully checked the notes she had
taken during her phone conversation with
Chrissy. Although the yard was mowed and the
curtains in the front window looked crisp and
white, there was a quiet atmosphere about the
house that just didn't fit in with her idea of the
social Sigma Thedas. But 124 was the number on
the slip of paper in her small clutch purse.

Taking a deep breath, she climbed the steps.
This was going to be one of the most important
hours in her college career.

A thin girl opened the front door. "Welcome.
I'm Betty."

Betty? Maybe things in Colorado didn't work
quite the way they did in San Francisco. Back
home, any popular girl named Betty would certainly have a cute nickname.

"I'm Caroline Kirby."

"Kirby?" Betty cocked her head to one side. "I
don't remember your name from our RSVP list."

"But I called," Caroline claimed. Things were
definitely not working out according to plan.
After the first frustrating conversation with
Chrissy, she'd decided not to call her cousin back
to get the Sigma Theda phone number. Instead,

she'd gotten the number from Student Services.

Betty smiled. "Come in anyway. Everyone is welcome."

Caroline raised her eyebrows and followed the girl into the house. *Everyone is welcome?* The Sigma Thedas were surprisingly democratic, considering their reputation.

No more than thirty girls were standing in the living room in quiet conversational groups. Caroline couldn't help touching her silk dress when she saw the others wearing simple blouses and dark skirts. She couldn't believe that she'd overdressed.

As soon as her initial feeling of panic had subsided, Caroline realized that something very strange was going on. Ellis was from Denver, and her fashionable wardrobe didn't include frilly white blouses. So why would girls at a party in Boulder be wearing such conservative, unstylish clothing?

Betty sat in the center of a plain cream-colored couch under the front window. "We can get started now that everyone is here. Cecily, please tell the freshman pledges about Alpha Theda."

Alpha Theda! She should have known better than to call Chrissy—that cousin of hers was the one guaranteed disaster in her life! The Sigma Theda party was the most important of her entire college career, and Chrissy was responsible for her missing it! Why hadn't she followed her instincts and stopped at the first sorority house that caught her attention? She glanced at the door and nearly cried out in frustration. Cecily loomed between her and freedom.

Cecily folded her hands and smiled at her sisters and the pledges. "As you know, we Alpha Thedas are proud of our contributions to the community. Several times a year we donate money to deserving causes. We earn money for these charities by serving at alumni dinners and other functions held on campus where we are paid minimum wage."

She paused for a moment, and Caroline wondered what Cecily could possibly add to this thrilling news. "For those of you who don't know, the highlight of first semester is our trip to downtown, during which we help cook Thanksgiving dinner for those less fortunate than ourselves." Cecily looked around the room at the potential Alpha Theda girls. "Are there any questions?"

Several hands popped into the air, but Caroline kept her question to herself. Chewing her lower lip, she wondered how she could kill her cousin without leaving a trace of evidence.

Caroline could not argue with the good intentions of the Alpha Theda sisters. Of course there should be students on campus who cared about the world around them. However, she didn't feel guilty in the least that she wasn't one of them. She didn't attend college to mash potatos on Thanksgiving or pour coffee for wealthy alumni. Checking her watch, she realized she had just enough time to stop by the Sigma Theda house.

She was sure it was the one she'd noticed on her way to 124 Aspen.

Chrissy leaned back in the modular chair and rested her tennis shoes on the matching footrest. She took a deep breath of the fresh air blowing through the open window overhead. Outside, the pine trees were gently rustling in the breeze. In her opinion, Buttler Library was a really comfortable place to work. She just hoped she could relax and study at the same time.

She flipped past the title page and squinted at page one of *Absalom, Absalom*. The print was so small a person could go blind reading it. Chrissy tried to concentrate but the rambling sentences made no sense. She was surprised to find that, as she neared the bottom of the page, she hadn't reached the end of the first sentence. One . . . two . . . three . . . The first sentence was fourteen lines long! And as far as she was concerned, the author was taking too long to describe an old lady sitting in a hot room.

Closing her eyes for a minute, Chrissy promised herself she would read the first four chapters. A sophomore had been nice enough to warn her about Professor Pauly's famous trick, and she intended to beat him at his own game. It wasn't fair for a teacher to quiz his students on the first day of class, expecting them to have read the full week's assignment by Monday morning. *I am not going to start my college career as a victim*, she vowed.

Determined to understand the story, she continued to stare at the page before her until it began to blur. She had no idea she was falling asleep until a shout outside the window woke her. Startled, she jumped up and her book flew out of her hands.

Standing up on her chair, Chrissy leaned toward the window to see what was happening. Outside, there had to be at least a dozen boys and girls tossing brightly colored Frisbees at each other. One went out of control and coasted close to the window. Even though a screen separated her from the Frisbee, she couldn't help reaching out for it.

"Hey!" a big sandy-haired guy called. "Are you being held captive in the library?"

Chrissy grinned and looked over her shoulder. "I think I could escape," she giggled.

"Then why don't you come out here and help my team win?" he asked.

"Really?" she said, thrilled at the prospect of escaping from *Absalom, Absalom*.

Chrissy stuffed the paperback book into her purse and headed outside. She had no problem finding her way around the side of the library to the Frisbee game. So far, getting around campus hadn't been half as complicated as she'd expected.

"I'm Chrissy," she told the guy who had invited her to join the game.

"I'm Jake." He shoved a blue Frisbee in her hand. Chrissy loved the feel of the sun on her face and the breeze in her hair. It reminded her of a lazy day back home in Iowa when all the work was done.

"You're pretty good," a girl with light brown hair said between tosses.

"Thanks. It feels great to be doing something outside."

"Do you like the mountains?" she asked.

"I think they're great. We don't have anything like them back in Iowa."

"Have you heard about the Climbing Club?"

"Ladies . . . ," Jake called out. "This isn't a social event. It's a serious game."

"My name's Nan," the girl whispered. "The Climbing Club meets tomorrow afternoon."

Chrissy had to jump to catch the Frisbee coming her way. She'd barely caught her balance after landing when someone grabbed her arm and pulled her away from the playing area. Chrissy was surprised by the strength of her cousin's grip.

"What's going on, Cara?" Chrissy asked, puzzled.

"Hey, Chrissy!" Jake said. "What are you doing? The game isn't over yet."

"I know, but my cousin wants to talk to me. I think you'll have to win the game without me."

"See you tomorrow!" Nan called out enthusiastically.

Caroline squinted at the players. "Who are they?"

"Well, the big guy is Jake Someone, and the girl is Nan."

"And everyone else?"

Chrissy could only shrug. "I have no idea."

"You just started playing Frisbee with a bunch of strangers?"

Sure her mom had taught her not to talk to strangers, but Chrissy didn't think that advice would apply to a bunch of people playing Frisbee in broad daylight on a college campus. "If you hadn't pulled me out of the game, I might have gotten to know a few of them. Then they wouldn't be strangers."

"I happen to have a very good reason for pulling you out of the game," Caroline said in a huffy tone. "I wanted to go to the *Sigma* Theda tea, but you sent me to the *Alpha* Theda house."

"Sigma? Alpha?" Chrissy couldn't help laughing. "They're all Greek to me."

She expected her cousin to groan over the bad joke she'd made, but Caroline just planted her hands on her hips and steamed. Her lips were pursed, and her blue eyes were shooting sparks.

Chrissy did her best to look apologetic. "I didn't mean to wreck your day or anything."

"Whether you meant to or not, you probably just ruined my whole college career!" Caroline growled.

"Be serious, Cara," she insisted. Her cousin had to be exaggerating. "Nothing could be that bad."

Caroline stuck out her stubborn chin. "Yes, it could. The Sigmas are the most prestigious sorority on campus. The Alphas feed dinner to the poor—"

"That's nice." Chrissy was confused. Was her cousin really this fried over some girls' club with a funny name?

"With the Sigmas I would have gotten to know all the right people," Caroline began in sober tones. "I would have been invited to the best parties. And I'd probably have great job contacts when I graduate. But you had to send me to Alpha Theda, where I would have spent four years of college learning to be a waitress."

"You're not exactly making sense," Chrissy warned.

Caroline pressed a hand to her forehead. "The details don't matter. All I know is that you trashed my life today."

"Why don't you see the Sigmas another day?" When Caroline sucked in her breath, Chrissy knew she had hit a nerve.

"I stopped by the Sigma house after I escaped the Alphas," Caroline explained very slowly, "but it seems that Sigmas never make mistakes. In fact, I'm not sure those girls are even human."

"They were rude to you," Chrissy concluded bluntly.

"They made me feel like an idiot for thinking someone who couldn't show up at the right address could be a Sigma Theda."

Chrissy was confused. "If they're so nasty, why are you so upset that you can't be one of them?"

Caroline shook her head. "They're not nasty to

everyone—just to freshmen who show up an hour late and beg for a chance to stay."

"You begged?" Chrissy couldn't imagine her perfect cousin throwing herself on anyone's mercy.

She hung her head. "I didn't mean to, but I would have done anything to pledge with them. Don't you see? If you had given me the right address, I would have stopped at the right house and I'd be on my way to joining the best sorority on campus at this very moment."

"I'm sorry." Chrissy hadn't given her cousin the wrong information on purpose. Still, she hated to see her cousin so miserable.

"I wish 'sorry' could fix things, but it can't."

"I know," Chrissy desperately wanted Caroline to lighten up. "But now you must understand how much I'm going to need your help with French class."

"What does that have to do with the sorority?"

Chrissy ventured a smile. "If I'm that bad with two Greek words, you can imagine what I'll do to the whole French language!"

Caroline shook her head, grinning in spite of herself. "You'll probably start a war."

Chapter 6

"Chrissy, in here!" Nan called from a classroom in the science building.

Since Chrissy didn't know anyone else in the room, she headed for the girl from the Frisbee game who had also turned up in her biology class that morning. "Is this the Climbing Club?"

"It sure is. I saved you a seat." Nan pointed to the empty desk next to her.

Chrissy dropped her books on the desk and slid into the seat. "I was so glad to be in your biology class this morning!"

"Is our class special or something?" Nan asked.

"Compared to Biology one-oh-oh-one, it's great!"

"One-oh-oh-one?" Nan asked, confused.

"Yeah. The woman at registration punched an

extra zero in her computer. At eight o'clock this morning I had to march into a class of certified brains and ask for a class-change card."

Nan winced. "It sounds horrible."

"Staying in the senior class would have been worse," she confided. "How do you like Intro to Bio so far?"

"I'm not worried about the classes, but a two-hour lab session every week . . ." Nan rolled her eyes.

"Want to be my partner for the bug hunt on Thursday?" The teacher had talked about their exploring the ecosystem beyond their classroom, but it sounded like a bug hunt to Chrissy.

"I have to warn you," Nan said with a crooked grin. "I'm terrified of spiders."

"I'll take the spiders, if you scare away the snakes."

"It's a deal." Nan tried to push her short brown hair behind her ears, but her curls seemed to have a mind of their own. "Hey, you're taking French."

"I'm attempting to take French," Chrissy corrected her new friend.

"*Parlez-vous français?*" Nan inquired.

"*Non.*" It was the only word Chrissy remembered from class, and she knew she was going to have to do a lot better in the future.

"Don't worry about it," Nan advised. "It'll get easier. What else are you taking?"

"American government and American literature."

"Sounds patriotic," Nan teased. "Do you like your classes?"

"I don't have my first political-science class until tomorrow, and my English class will probably be all right, but . . ."

"Your teacher is a gorgeous guy and you can't think about books around him?"

"I wish." Professor Pauly was a round, middle-aged man who looked more like someone's father than a college professor.

"Then what's wrong with your class?"

"I fell for a practical joke," Chrissy admitted. "Some sophomore told me Professor Pauly gives a test on the first day of class to see if any of his students have read the week's assignment. I stayed up until two o'clock this morning trying to read over a hundred pages—"

"And there wasn't any test?" Nan guessed.

Chrissy sighed. "I fell for the scam like a—"

"Like a freshman!" Nan finished. "You can't help it. You're new on campus."

"I bet you haven't done anything that stupid," Chrissy said.

"But I've got an older brother around to help me. Remember Jake from the Frisbee game?"

"Okay! Let's get started." Chrissy turned her attention to the front of the room. A boy with dark hair and a red bandanna was standing behind the desk. "I'm Frank Devine, president of the Climbing Club. If you're looking for the Needlepoint League, you're in the wrong place."

Chrissy giggled and a boy two desks ahead of

Chrissy looked over his shoulder to see who was laughing. She felt her cheeks turn red immediately when she saw him. He had a face that belonged to a man in a magazine ad for a Jeep— rugged but very handsome. When he winked at her, Chrissy's breath caught in her throat.

Frank explained that the club had a weekend trip planned to Roosevelt National Forest. He apologized for it's not being a challenging adventure, but in the fall they had to stay closer to campus. Early snowstorms in the mountains could be dangerous and they didn't want to risk losing any new campers who came along on the trip. He promised there would be an exciting trip to Rocky Mountain National Park in the spring.

"Anyone interested in this weekend's trip needs to sign up today so we can pack enough food," he said.

"I thought we were going to catch our own fish and fry them over a campfire," one club member said.

"We hope to catch enough for the group, but we don't want anyone starving up on the trail just because the fishing was bad." A few people laughed. "Plus, it takes six months to get a Colorado fishing license."

Chrissy and Nan groaned in unison. Nan leaned over and whispered, "Either we find someone who'll share their fish or we're going to be eating peanut-butter-and-jelly sandwiches all weekend."

In spite of the threat of starvation, Chrissy followed Nan to the desk where they signed up for the trip. When someone tapped her firmly on her shoulder, Chrissy turned and found herself staring at the ruggedly handsome man she'd noticed earlier.

"You're new," he said with an easy smile that sent a shiver down Chrissy's spine.

"Yes." She was glad he hadn't asked her a more difficult question.

"I'm Joe Thornton." His hands in his pockets, he rocked back on his heels. "Welcome to the club."

"Thanks. I'm Chrissy Madden." She felt like she should shake hands or something. Luckily his hands were buried in his pockets because hers were embarrassingly damp.

"Have you camped before, Chrissy?" he asked, his brown eyes sparkling as he spoke.

"Not in the mountains." She'd spent a lot of time outdoors, but she didn't know a thing about mountain climbing.

He sat on the edge of a desk. "Even if we don't do anything as challenging as climbing Mount Everest, do you think you could use some advice?"

"Definitely." Chrissy hoped it wasn't obvious when she swallowed hard. She'd accept any help he had to offer.

Joe looked over her head. "Hey, Frank! Could I get an equipment list for Chrissy?"

He motioned for her to stand next to him while he reviewed the items she would need for the weekend trip. Chrissy knew she'd have to study the sheet later on, when she was alone. Being this close to Joe made her brain feel scrambled. When he pointed to the suggested brands of backpacks, she saw his hands instead of the names. When he told her she'd need a hat to protect her fair skin, she gazed at his ruddy cheeks.

"A tent is a big investment for someone who might not keep climbing," he said. "A lot of people share."

Chrissy's heart beat wildly. Was he asking her to share his tent?

"You should check around with some of the girls before too many people leave," he suggested.

"Yeah. That's a good idea," she mumbled, mortified by her overactive imagination. She took the list without meeting his warm eyes. "Thanks."

He gave her a toothy grin. "You're very welcome."

"Thornton!" someone called. "Are you working out today?"

"I'll be right there." He raised a hand to stall his friends. Giving Chrissy his full attention, he asked, "Will I see you Saturday?"

Like an idiot, Chrissy nodded and watched him leave. He had to be over six feet tall. She couldn't say for sure, but he looked like he was all muscle.

"I've got a tent to share," Nan offered. "Since Jake's playing football this season, I've got custody of our family tent."

"That's nice . . . ," Chrissy murmured, preferring her fantasies to Nan's practical suggestions.

"Earth to Chrissy," Nan teased. "I know he's gorgeous, but Joe's one of my brother's friends. They're both juniors."

"A junior?" Nan might as well have said he was a teacher. Chrissy told herself she should forget about him. What junior would want to hang around with a freshman? Especially a junior as handsome and friendly as Joe.

"Hi, Cara. How was your first day of classes?" Chrissy asked her cousin.

Caroline groaned and laid her head down on the open book on her desk. "Don't ask."

"She's up to her eyeballs in culture," Ellis remarked.

"That's nothing new," Chrissy said. Caroline was always involved in something artistic. In addition to her father's music and her mother's art, she had studied ballet for years.

"I have tons of reading to do," Caroline complained.

"Art history isn't going to be that bad," Ellis told her.

"You have a class together?" Chrissy didn't want to be jealous of Ellis, but it just didn't seem right. Caroline had a class with her roommate— but none with her own cousin!

"Yeah." Ellis didn't seem to notice Chrissy's distress. "We watch films, look at prints, and write a couple of papers."

"The professor has heard of my mother's gallery, and she's expecting wonderful work from me." Caroline got up from her chair and flopped on her bed. "I also have to read fifty pages for European history by Wednesday. And we're going to read ten novels in French literature."

"In French? The books are all in French?"

Caroline nodded.

Chrissy sat on the foot of the bed. "That sounds terrible. It would take me all four years of college to finish them."

Caroline laughed softly, trying to imagine her cousin struggling through just one foreign-language novel.

"Only biology looks easy—except for the labs," she said. "You got into the right biology class, didn't you?"

"You're not taking that super-brain class?" Ellis inquired.

"No." Chrissy said proudly, "I just went into the class and explained what had happened. The teacher wrote something on a form and told me to take it back to the registration desk. I only had to wait in line for forty-five minutes."

"I swear we're going to spend more time waiting around on lines than learning anything in this place," Ellis moaned.

Caroline didn't seem to hear the complaint, or else she'd heard it too many times to pay any attention. "How is your biology class?"

"Fine. Nan Sanderson and I are going to be lab partners."

"Who's Nan?" Caroline asked.

"I met her Sunday afternoon outside the library." Chrissy was careful not to mention anything about the sorority-tea mix-up.

"She was one of the Frisbee players?" Caroline guessed.

"The short one with curly brown hair. She invited me to the Climbing Club today," Chrissy explained.

"The Climbing Club?" Caroline sat up, supporting herself on her elbows.

"Yeah. We're going to take camping trips in the mountains. In fact, I'm spending the weekend in Roosevelt National Forest." She lifted her right leg and held out her foot. "How do you like my hiking boots? I bought them right after dinner."

"But why?" Ellis was staring as though the boots were hideous, live creatures. "Why would you want to buy something that ugly?"

"It's hard to climb mountains in high heels," Chrissy said, managing to keep a straight face.

"You're really going to climb a mountain?" Ellis inspected her long nails. It was obvious she wouldn't climb a mountain if her life depended on it; she might ruin her manicure.

"It's more like hiking and camping out for the night," Chrissy explained. After all, she didn't want her cousin worrying about her.

"Hiking and camping," Caroline said in a sarcastic voice that Chrissy would have expected from Ellis.

"It'll be fun," said Chrissy defensively.

"Fun. You came to college just to have fun?" Caroline inquired.

"Sure. College doesn't have to be all hard work."

"When are you going to grow up?" Caroline's voice grew louder. "Didn't you come to college to learn?"

Chrissy stood to back away from her cousin's anger. "I'm learning lots of things," Chrissy claimed. "But there's more to life than what's in your books!"

"Of course." Caroline calmed down a bit. "We can learn a lot from the people we meet—that's why it's important to meet the right people. What connections are a bunch of hikers going to have?

Chrissy glared at her cousin. "What I've learned so far is that they like me the way I am."

"Listen, Chrissy, I just want you to make the best of what college has to offer," Caroline claimed.

"That's what I'm trying to do."

"But you can't go around joining every club that sounds like fun. You have to be more careful about your choices," Caroline insisted.

"Give it up," Ellis advised. "Your cousin can't appreciate your excellent advice."

"And you wouldn't appreciate fun if it slapped you in the face!" Chrissy told Ellis before she turned and stalked out of the room.

It doesn't matter what Caroline thinks, she told herself on her walk back to Culver Hall. So far, college was going very well. Her classes were interesting, and she'd made a few friends.

She hoped things were going well for Caroline. Her cousin really seemed buried in homework. And Ellis was going to drive away any nice person who wanted to get to know her cousin. But she knew she shouldn't worry. Things would work out for Caroline.

She smiled to herself. Two months ago she wouldn't have been able to imagine herself strolling across the lawn at Colorado University after her first day of classes. In spite of the warnings from Caroline and Ellis, Chrissy had a feeling that college was going to be great fun.

Chapter 7

"You know, in a crazy way I envy Chrissy," Caroline confided after her cousin had left.

"You? *You're* jealous of *her*?" Ellis's dark eyes widened. "Why?"

"She seems to be fitting in so easily . . . and she's so happy."

"Let's look at this carefully." Ellis grabbed a pen and a notebook. "How is she fitting in easily?"

"On Sunday she was playing Frisbee with a bunch of strangers. I don't know how she got into the game, but I could never talk to people I didn't know—let alone ask if I could be on their team."

"Of course, you couldn't. And there is nothing wrong with that," Ellis said, sounding like a psychiatrist. "You are more selective. Caroline Kirby *does not* pick up strangers."

"That's true, but I'll be up to my eyebrows in books this weekend, while she's off in the mountains having fun."

"The Climbing Club," Ellis snorted. "Caroline, what's she going to get out of spending the night in a sleeping bag except cold feet? You're smart enough to know that the right clubs can make a difference."

"And while I wait to find the right club, Chrissy's going to be having tons of fun." Caroline sighed. It was always that way between them—Chrissy had fun while she worried.

"You have to keep your eye on the future. Who will be happier in the long run?"

Caroline couldn't tell her roommate that Chrissy would be happy anywhere. Her cousin landed on her feet in every situation. "But I don't have any idea what club is right anymore. I wish I could have been a Sigma Theda," Caroline said sadly.

"You're not jealous of Chrissy. You're just depressed," Ellis concluded.

"And why shouldn't I be? What's more important than starting college with the right connections?"

Ellis nodded in agreement. "Nothing's more important."

"With the Sigma Thedas, I would have had the perfect image. Who else can do that for me?"

"The Music Society," Ellis said, smiling smugly.

Caroline noticed the look on her roommate's face and wondered for a moment if this was some kind of joke. "The Music Society?"

"Not many people know about the group, but it is *the* place to meet the right people," Ellis confided.

"Why haven't I heard of it?"

"It's an elite group," she explained. "You have to be invited to join."

"Great." If she hadn't been good enough for the Sigma Thedas, how could Caroline expect to be invited to join the Music Society?

"I can try to get you in," Ellis said.

"How can you do that?" Caroline couldn't believe a freshman would have much influence in a private club. "In fact, how do you even know about the Music Society?"

"I know three upperclassmen in the society from home."

Caroline raised her eyebrows. She and Ellis hadn't talked about their families much, but Ellis must have traveled in the right circles in Denver if she knew three members.

"There's a meeting tomorrow night. Would you like to come as my guest?"

"I'd like that very much," Caroline told her roommate. "Any friend of yours is a friend of mine."

Caroline sat on a platform covered with plush navy carpeting and smoothed her borrowed black silk pants over her thighs. She hadn't been sure about wearing the pants and glittery top when Ellis offered to lend them to her, but she could see she was dressed appropriately for the occasion. She really felt like she belonged in the room, unlike at the Alpha Theda fiasco. Apparently they held a reception for themselves in the music-building lobby each fall. Everyone was dressed dramatically, but tastefully, in clothes and jewelry that spelled money with a capital *M*.

"Paul, I'd like you to meet my roommate Caroline Kirby," Ellis told a tall boy with blond hair that almost covered his intense eyes.

"Kirby . . ." He seemed to be mulling over her name.

"Any relation to Cissy Kirby?" a girl with long auburn hair asked. "She was my roommate sophomore year at Broadmoor."

"You're a transfer to C.U.?" Caroline asked, anxious to meet someone else who was new to the society.

Paul chuckled.

"Hardly," the girl said, "Broadmoor is a boarding school north of London."

"Of course." Caroline tried to pretend it had been a silly mistake on her part, but she didn't think she was fooling anyone. They all probably knew she had never heard of Broadmoor.

She noticed Paul pull Ellis aside, but she couldn't hear what he said to her roommate.

"Say, Will," someone called across the room. "Was that you in the silver Porsche?"

"It was," a good-looking boy behind Ellis affirmed. "Got it for my birthday last month."

"It's a hot car," the other guy commented.

Will nodded in agreement. "I know."

Caroline was happy to see that the people in this crowd acted more mature than the kids she'd known in high school. In high school, whenever one of them got a new car, everyone had to ride in it. Without actually saying so, Will had made it clear that rides in his new Porsche would be limited to a fortunate few.

"Where did you get the great tan, Annette?" Ellis asked the girl from Broadmoor.

"The Riviera," she said as casually as if she were mentioning the neighborhood pool down the street.

Caroline knew she shouldn't be so surprised. Her friends back in San Francisco spent summers in Europe, and she had traveled a lot with her parents. It wasn't so much where they had been, but how they talked about it that impressed her.

"Have you been abroad?" Paul asked Caroline.

"A few times. My parents travel for their business."

"You had to go with your family?" another girl asked. "What a drag. Parents don't know how to have fun."

A tall, slender man in a tweed sport coat cleared his throat. "Let's dispense with the formalities quickly, then we can continue catching up with one another."

"Good idea, Robert," a member called out.

"I see a few new faces. Why don't the members introduce themselves, and then the sponsors can introduce their guests." He adjusted his wire-rimmed glasses, and Caroline noticed the suede elbow patches on his jacket. She decided Robert must be a senior and president of the club.

Each member gave his name, class, and a short description of himself. Actually, Caroline noticed most of them talked about their families—their homes, yachts, and corporate positions. Very few had much to say about themselves short of where they had spent the summer.

Paul put his hand on Ellis's shoulder. "I'm sure everyone remembers Ellis Lattimore. Her mother hosted our dinner when we caught the London Symphony in Denver last spring."

Several members complimented the Lattimore home and the five-course catered meal. To Caroline's surprise, none of them mentioned the concert.

"I think we all agree that Ellis will be a fine addition to our group," Annette said, tossing her long auburn hair over her shoulder.

Robert spoke up. "Please save your comments until we vote later."

Paul turned his attention to Caroline. "Ellis has brought along her roommate, Caroline Kirby. I'm afraid I don't know much about her."

"Miss Kirby, would you like to introduce yourself?" Robert, the group leader, requested.

When Ellis had invited her, Caroline had thought her friend would smooth the way for her somehow. How was she supposed to impress these people with her background?

"I'm from San Francisco. My father, Richard Kirby, is a music critic. Perhaps some of you have read his column. . . ."

"Seriously, your father's actually a music critic?" Will sounded amused by the idea of someone at the meeting having any real involvement in music.

"I'm from San Francisco. I know about your family," the red headed guy behind Will said, much to Caroline's relief. "Your mom is Edith Kirby. She owns that wonderful new art gallery, right?"

Modesty almost made Caroline hesitate before agreeing that her mother's gallery *was* wonderful. Then she remembered how everyone else had spoken so highly of themselves. "Right. That's my family," she told him, sounding more confident than she felt.

When all of the visitors had been introduced, Robert moved on to the next order of business. "We need to discuss fall activities."

"Dinner at Henry's was fun last year," Annette said.

"You thought so?" Paul inquired. "I thought the strolling violins were a nuisance."

"Dinners and parties are fine, but I was hoping we could decide on one big event," interjected Richard. "There is a touring production of *The Marriage of Figaro* coming to Denver in October."

"What about a weekend in New York—we could catch a few Broadway plays," Paul suggested.

Caroline wanted to ask how they could possibly afford such a trip, but she bit her tongue. She knew her parents weren't going to understand when she asked for enough money to cover a weekend of dining and theater in New York.

"That's possible between semesters or over vacation," Robert allowed. "Anyone who's interested can meet with you about planning a trip to New York."

"The Figaro thing sounds fine," Will told him. "I know we have to do something musical each semester to qualify as the campus Music Society."

"He's right," Annette said with a sigh. "It will do."

"In that case, I'll work on the details and get back to you. That's it for tonight's business," Robert concluded.

As the others divided into small groups to talk, Caroline bit her lip and wondered what she should do. Ellis was laughing with her friends, the upperclassmen from Denver. She didn't feel right about walking up to Annette or Will and joining in their discussions.

Robert also was alone, and she felt nervous as he began to walk toward her. She hoped he wasn't going to ask her to leave.

"So, Caroline Kirby, what did you think of our first meeting? I'm Robert Winston, the graduate student advisor for the society." He pushed his brown hair away from his forehead in a way that made Caroline's heart stop for just the merest second.

"I thought you were the society president."

He smiled broadly. "This group doesn't have official officers." When he saw Caroline's confused look, he tried to explain why the society was unique. "Some people say there isn't a student president because no one in this group wants to work that hard. Others claim it would be silly to have a president of a group whose purpose is purely social."

"I like the second explanation better," she told him. While Caroline felt uncomfortable about joining a group of lazy students, she found the idea of socializing with all the best people on campus to be very appealing.

"Why?" he inquired.

"You sound like a teacher," Caroline laughed.

"I am a graduate assistant in the music department. I teach some of the introductory classes."

Caroline felt herself blushing, but decided to tell him the truth even though it was embarrassing. "At first I thought you were a senior. But I should have known you were older than any of the other students here."

"Robert," Paul called, his arm casually thrown around Ellis's shoulder. "We're going to La Maison Rouge. Want to join us?"

"Sure. Are visitors invited, too?" he asked.

Paul looked down at Ellis. "I thought we could all have dessert and coffee. Afterward, the hopefuls will have to leave so we can decide who will be joining the society this fall."

"Are you coming?" Robert asked Caroline.

It sounded like she had to go with the group. If she left, they might get the wrong idea and not invite her to join. Her European-history assignment would have to wait. "Of course."

"La Maison Rouge is a French Restaurant on the edge of town," he said as they walked to her car. "They have the most sinful desserts in the whole state of Colorado."

"It sounds wonderful," she said. "The cafeteria food is decent, but the cream puffs leave something to be desired."

Robert's deep laugh made her smile. "I think they add a pinch of lead to the pastry to make it so heavy," he quipped.

"So you eat at the dining hall also?" She asked.

"Only when my kitchen is empty," he told her as he stopped next to a blue MG. "I have an apartment off campus."

Caroline pinched herself, trying to convince herself she wasn't dreaming. After worrying that she wouldn't fit in on campus, she'd stumbled into heaven, thanks to Ellis. The next hour or so at La Maison Rouge was the only thing that could keep her from success. If she was able to keep the chocolate sauce from drooling down her chin, she'd be joining the society along with Ellis. And then she'd see a lot more of Robert Winston.

Chapter 8

"Did you understand one word of that movie?" Chrissy asked Denise as they walked toward Culver Hall.

"No." Denise shook her head. "The French dialogue flew by, and the English subtitles didn't seem to have anything to do with what was happening on the screen."

"So why do you think Madame Carson told everyone in French one-oh-one to see the movie?"

"Maybe she wanted to inspire us to study hard so we can appreciate the next French film shown on campus," Denise suggested.

The film hadn't inspired Chrissy in the least. If anything, it had made her worry about how she was going to pass her French class if Caroline was too busy to help her.

"What's your favorite class so far?" Denise asked, walking rapidly to keep up with Chrissy.

"Political science," she answered without hesitation. "Professor Barker makes it so exciting. For example, today we were talking about the Iran-Contra scandal from 1987. He started telling us about how he thought Ollie North was a hero. When no one argued with him, he slapped his hands on his head and screamed, "Think, people! Think!"

"That's exciting? Was he trying to convince you Ollie North was a hero? Or was he angry that no one argued with him because he thinks the guy isn't a hero?" Denise shook her head.

"He never told us what he really believes," Chrissy explained. "He wants us to think for ourselves. He says we shouldn't buy everything he says any more than we should believe one hundred percent of what Dan Rather says on the nightly news."

"Oh, I get it!" Denise said. "Do you have tons of homework in his class or is it mostly discussion?"

"Are you thinking of transferring into Barker's class?" Chrissy asked.

"I should. I'm going to fail my calculus test tomorrow morning unless I study half the night."

"I'll stay up with you," Chrissy volunteered as they walked up the four flights of stairs to their room. "I got some articles at the library today for my political-science paper that I'd like to start reading."

"So you do have homework for that class," Denise concluded.

"We have to research a current government controversy. I picked the day-care dilemma. Should the government be regulating child care more carefully, or is it a person's right to raise their children without intervention?"

"Sounds like you know a lot about it already," Denise said.

"Those aren't my words," Chrissy was quick to explain. "He handed out a list of topics, and I picked one."

Chrissy unlocked the door and headed for her desk to show Denise all the information she had found on her topic. "Where did I leave my stuff?"

"What stuff?" asked Denise.

"I wanted to show you the research materials I found at the library for my paper." Chrissy checked her desk drawer, but the articles weren't there. She looked under the bottom bunk, but there was nothing there except dust.

"Where did you get the red ski cap?" Denise asked. Is it something for the camping trip?"

"I don't have a red ski cap," Chrissy said, pulling her head out from underneath the bed.

"Oh no! Look at this!" Denise cried.

Chrissy took the hat from her roommate and read the note that was pinned to it.

Chrissy Madden, If you ever want to see your library books and photocopied articles again, make sure this hat is on Elmer Frame's head by seven o'clock tomorrow morning.

The Freshman Stalker of Culver Hall

"Your articles have been kidnapped!" Denise exclaimed. "Who can we call for help?"

"No one." The ransom note didn't mention the authorities, but Chrissy had seen enough movies to know the thief would torch her research materials if she called campus security.

"Isn't Elmer Frame that ugly statue in front of the Student Union?" Denise asked.

"Yeah. The one that's about a hundred feet tall." How was she going to get the hat up on Elmer's stone head? Chrissy wondered, beginning to panic.

Denise touched the red wool hat. "I'll help you."

Although Chrissy wanted to accept the offer, she refused. "You can't. You have to study for your calculus test."

"But what will you do?" Denise asked, sounding relieved.

"I guess I'll have to call my cousin," Chrissy said slowly. Considering the way Caroline had been acting since she met Ellis, Chrissy wasn't convinced that her cousin would want to help her. But finally she decided she had nothing to lose by asking—Caroline wouldn't leave her in a lurch at a time like this.

* * *

Halfway to the Student Union, Caroline asked herself why she was sneaking around campus at four-thirty in the morning. When she left home for college she thought she'd outgrown all the weird crazy stuff she had done with her friends at Maxwell High. And the stunts had all started when Chrissy came to live with her family.

"So why am I surprised that I'm out with the owls and the bats?" she whispered to herself. As long as Chrissy was around, no one knew what would happen next.

"There you are," Chrissy said softly.

"I thought you'd changed your mind."

"Maybe I should have," Caroline said once she got a good look at how tall Elmer Frame really was. Although she had seen the statue several times, she had never considered climbing it before this morning.

"I like your outfit," Chrissy said, in an obvious attempt to improve Caroline's mood. "I thought it was appropriate." Caroline was determined not to be swayed by Chrissy's compliment.

"Your cat-burglar black sweater and leggings are much smarter than my jeans and red sweat shirt."

"You *are* almost glowing in the dark," Caroline admitted.

Chrissy shrugged and pulled something out from under her shirt. "Here's the stocking cap."

"I'd like to get this over with." Caroline looked over her shoulder, but there wasn't a person anywhere in sight. "I don't want to be here when people start heading for breakfast."

"Neither do I," Chrissy agreed.

"How do you plan to do the deed?" Caroline inquired. It was her cousin's problem, and she hoped Chrissy had thought of a strategy.

"I was thinking you could climb on my shoulder—"

"Why me?" Caroline burst out. "It isn't my class project being held hostage. Why should I have to climb the statue?"

"You're the ex-ballerina. That makes you the limber one."

"Okay, Chrissy, just give me the hat." Caroline tucked it inside her sleeve. She didn't want it getting in her way.

"I thought you could get onto my shoulders by climbing up on the base," Chrissy instructed.

The granite base was higher than her waist. Caroline needed a boost to get a foothold. She grabbed Elmer's shin and pulled herself up on the flat stone. From the position, she was able to get onto Chrissy's shoulders easily.

"This isn't going to work," she told her partner. "I can only reach Elmer's shoulder. There's no way I can get this hat on his head."

"What now?" Chrissy said.

"The base is really wide. You could come up here, too."

Caroline carefully dropped off Chrissy's shoulders onto the stone, and then helped her cousin scramble up to the same level. This time it was trickier to get onto Chrissy's shoulders. Chrissy squatted a bit, and Caroline grabbed Elmer's lowered hand.

"I thought you could jump," Chrissy teased.

"We never did our ballet lessons on a statue," Caroline replied, trying to keep her hands from slipping off Elmer's bronze palm.

"What's happening?" Chrissy asked, unsure of how much longer she could support Caroline's weight.

"If you can stand up, I think I can reach."

Groaning from the strain of trying to keep her balance while lifting her cousin, Chrissy straightened her legs and lifted Caroline higher. "Better?"

"I'm staring at his chin," she reported. "Hold tight while I get the hat out of my sleeve." The last thing they needed was for her to lose her balance. "I think I've got it!" Caroline said.

"I'll be careful while you reach for his head."

Caroline rested one hand on Elmer's shoulder and stood up tall but she couldn't quite reach far enough to pull the hat down over Elmer's head. Taking a deep breath, she firmly gripped one edge of the hat and tried to toss it at his head, hoping it would catch on somehow.

"Is it on his head yet?" Chrissy asked.

"Not yet." She tossed the hat over Elmer's head once more, still holding on to one edge. This time it caught. She leaned her body against Mr. Frame's shoulder and prayed to keep her balance while she used both hands to tug the hat low enough on his head so the first breeze wouldn't send it flying.

"It's done!" Caroline called.

"All right!"

Caroline gazed over her shoulder. "Oh, no!"

"Don't look down," Chrissy instructed, sensing that Caroline was losing her balance.

Chrissy's got it all wrong, Caroline thought as panic overwhelmed her. It wasn't the height she found unsettling, but the man who was jogging toward the Student Union.

Even though the morning light was dim and she was too far up to see his face clearly, she had a sinking feeling in her stomach that she knew who the jogger was. Caroline hoped he wouldn't notice the two of them glued to the statue. That hope diminished when she remembered Chrissy's bright red sweat shirt.

"Caroline? Is that you?" he asked.

She tried to smile. After all, Robert Winston was used to the Music Society members who never lost their cool. "Good morning, Robert."

"I didn't know you lived in Culver Hall," he said.

"She doesn't but I do," Chrissy explained.

Caroline figured he was wondering who the bottom half of their team was, so she made a quick introduction before Chrissy could say anything else. "Robert, this is my cousin Chrissy Madden."

"Nice to meet you, Chrissy. I'm Robert Winston."

"I'd shake hands, but . . ." Chrissy's shoulders started to shake when she giggled over her predicament.

"Don't laugh," Caroline whispered.

"What valuable item did the Stalker steal from you?" he asked Chrissy.

"My notes for a political-science paper."

"Hmm. That sounds serious, but not half as bad as last year. The Stalker used to snatch diaries and hot letters from boyfriends back home."

"How embarrassing!" Chrissy exclaimed.

"Do you think I could get down now?" Caroline asked, afraid the two of them were having so much fun that they'd forgotten her.

"Sure," Chrissy announced, bending her knees.

Caroline let her hands slide from Elmer's shoulder to his elbow. Chrissy took a step to one side and Caroline felt herself falling.

"Oh, no!" she cried out. It was impossible to hold on to Elmer's hand, the palm was worn smooth from years of being beaten by the wind and rain. She closed her eyes and faced the fact that she was going to fall in a heap at Robert's feet.

"I've got you!" he called out.

Robert didn't actually catch her in his arms, but he did break her fall. He managed to grab her flying arms and help her regain her balance.

"Thanks." Caroline tried to smile, but she felt too tense. "You probably saved my life."

"You're brave to be helping your cousin this way," Robert said soothingly.

"Yeah, Cara," Chrissy interrupted. "I didn't know we'd be risking our lives."

"Well, now that I've rescued a beautiful damsel in distress, I'm off to finish my run," said Robert as he jogged off. "See you later, Caroline!"

Caroline waited until Robert was out of sight before she turned on Chrissy. "Thanks a bunch! You just embarrassed me in front of one of the most interesting men on campus."

"I didn't know . . . I guess I should have kept my mouth shut." Chrissy grinned in her special way that made it impossible for Caroline to stay angry.

"We should get back to our dorms before anyone else finds us out here," said Caroline, trying hard not to smile. "Besides, what if it's against school rules to climb Elmer?"

Chrissy suddenly laughed. "Do you know what? My dorm is just as special as yours."

"What are you talking about?"

"Remember I was jealous of Fielding Hall's annual welcome-home party for upperclassmen? Well, now we know Culver has a tradition, too. The Stalker! And I was the person he or she chose. I'm honored!"

"Honored?" Caroline knew there were times it was wisest not to try to understand the way her cousin's brain worked. "I'm happy for you, Chrissy. But next time I think you should share the honor with someone else."

"You're right," Chrissy said, missing the point entirely. "I'll let Denise in on it next time."

Caroline shook her head in dismay. "You do that, Chrissy." Four years of college with Chrissy seemed like a very long time right now.

Chapter 9

"Hey Chrissy!"

Her hiking boots stopped in their tracks as if they had a mind of their own when Chrissy saw Joe Thornton. She whispered to Nan, "What do you think he wants?"

Her partner shrugged her shoulders. "Ask him yourself. He's heading our way."

Joe stopped a few feet from them and read her *I Luv San Francisco* T-shirt out loud. "You look great," he said, "but I hope you packed something a little warmer."

Chrissy had checked her list several times. Patting the pack on her back she said, "I've even got a wool shirt with me in case it turns cold."

He used his hand to shade his brown eyes as he

gazed at the clear blue sky. "I doubt we're going to freeze on our hike this afternoon."

"Everyone ready?" Frank Devine hollered to the scattered hikers. "Since we'll be moving along at different speeds, let's plan to regroup where the trail loops back to the main road. That way no one will be left behind on the trail when the rest of us meet back at the vans."

Chrissy looked at Nan with slight alarm. No one had mentioned anything about hikers getting stranded.

"Don't worry," Joe whispered. "I won't let you get lost."

"And if anyone gets light-headed from the elevation, please let your partner know," the club president continued. "If someone faints, the rest of us are going to have to carry you."

Chrissy patted Nan's shoulder. "I won't make you carry me."

"What about me?" Joe inquired. "What are you ladies going to do if I faint?"

Chrissy was speechless when she realized Joe intended to hike with them. Nan punched him in the arm. "I guess we'd just have to drag you out by your feet," she quipped.

The trail began with a steep incline, and the hikers in good shape immediately went on ahead of the others. Chrissy guessed Joe could easily keep up with the experienced hikers, but he seemed to want to walk with them.

"I can walk with someone else," Nan whispered to Chrissy when it became obvious that Joe was going to stay with them for the entire trip.

Chrissy didn't know what to tell her friend. On the one hand she wanted to be alone with Joe, even if she couldn't quite believe that he'd stay with her for the whole hike. On the other hand, she felt more secure with Nan there, because she seemed to know what to say to Joe when her own brain went numb.

"Don't you like me, Nan?" Joe teased her. Chrissy groaned inwardly—she couldn't believe Joe had overheard Nan's comment.

"Sure I like you," she told him. "But haven't you heard three's a crowd?"

He raised his eyebrows. "I think the more the merrier. Stay with us, Nan."

Chrissy smiled at her friend to let her know it was all right.

"Look up there!" Joe pointed to a large bird circling high overhead. "It's a hawk."

"I hope he's watching some little mouse instead of us hikers," Chrissy joked.

"He wouldn't be interested in us," he assured her, as if she didn't know about hawks from growing up in the country.

They reached the top of the hill and Chrissy was speechless. There were no words to describe the panoramic view before them. To their right the hill dropped off sharply, giving them a clear view of the majestic mountains beyond the tall pine forest. The bright sun made the yellow and orange leaves of the aspens shimmer. Already there was snow on the distant mountain peaks.

Suddenly Joe put an arm around Chrissy's shoulder and pointed down the hill. The unexpected contact made Chrissy's heart thud in her chest. Its rapid beating sent blood rushing to her brain until her head was spinning. She had no idea what he wanted her to see in the woods below them, until three magnificent elk came into view.

"They're so big!" she said, hoping she didn't sound like an idiot.

Joe laughed softly. More hikers appeared and Joe signaled for them to be quiet so they wouldn't frighten the animals. He pointed through the pines at the elks, and then he motioned for the girls to move ahead on the trail.

"Do you think they saw us?" Nan asked him.

"No," Joe said. "If they sensed our presence, they would have run away.

Chrissy knew it was silly, but she didn't think anyone—not even an elk—could help noticing Joe. In the middle of this wonderful wilderness, she was more interested in him than nature. She couldn't care less whether he talked about the animals or what he ate for dinner last night; she just wanted him to stay with her and Nan.

They met the others at the loop in the trail sooner than she'd expected. The others were sitting on rocks, enjoying the sun and the snacks they'd brought with them.

"Here's a free rock," Joe said, gazing at Chrissy as he patted the spot next to him.

Chrissy sat down on the boulder, so excited she

thought she might hyperventilate or something. She didn't know if her light head was from the altitude or Joe. Trying to mind her own business long enough to catch her breath, she unzipped her pack and took out her snack.

"What have you got?" He tried to grab her hand and Chrissy's pulse soared into the danger zone again.

"It's just a chocolate granola bar," she croaked. "What do you have?"

"Dried fruit. How is your chocolate?"

She peeled off the wrapper. "Melted."

"That's why I brought dried banana chips. Want some?"

"You'd share your snack with someone dumb enough not to know that chocolate melts on a hike?" She couldn't take his snack. What if he fainted on the way back to the vans as he'd threatened? She knew he was probably joking, but she and Nan couldn't possibly carry him to the end of the trail.

"I always pack a lot." He opened the zip-locked bag and set it on his lap.

Her stomach growled, but Chrissy didn't know how she was going to reach across his body and dig into the bag on his lap without fainting. Avoiding any contact with him, she cautiously snatched one chip from the very top of the bag.

To her amazement, Joe seemed to understand her embarrassment. He set the open bag on his palm and offered it to her. "Take a handful."

"Thanks." Chrissy ducked her head, knowing

her face was turning red. She was touched by his thoughtfulness and mortified by her burning cheeks.

None of them said much on the second half of the hike, but Nan sighed when the vans came into the sight. "Civilization!"

"Didn't you like the hike?" Joe asked her.

"I loved it, but I'm out of shape," she told him. Chrissy silently agreed with her friend. The Climbing Club was going to entail a bit more exertion than she'd bargained for.

It was a short drive to the campsite at Peaceful Valley. As soon as the vans were unloaded, they divided up the duties. Joe was one of the people sent off to fish for that night's dinner. "Want to come with me?" he asked, grabbing Chrissy's wrist.

"I should help with the tents," she said half-heartedly.

"You can make up for it in the morning by helping pack the vans," he promised. "I want to show you how to fish."

"But I can't fish. I'm a freshman." She hated to do it, but she had to remind him she didn't meet the six-month student enrollment requirement for obtaining a fishing license.

"I know," he said as if it didn't matter one bit to him. "But you'll be able to help next spring if you watch me this fall. I'd like to show you how to fly-fish."

Chrissy couldn't resist such a tempting offer to

spend time with Joe. "Just let me get my hat," she said, smiling up at him.

"Don't forget a jacket. You'll be surprised how cold it can get up here when the sun goes down," he warned her.

Chrissy joined Joe minutes later with her wool shirt tied around her waist. He didn't say much as they walked along until he found just the right spot along the river. He eyed her brother's Chicago Cubs baseball cap while he pulled his wading boots up over his knees.

"Where are you from, Chrissy?"

She tried to get comfortable on a rock with a rough surface as Joe started out into the river. "My family has a farm in Danbury, Iowa."

He nodded, whipping the air overhead as he snapped his rod back and forth until enough line had been released. He cast his fake fly across the river. It landed on top of the water just below an overhanging rock.

"This is nothing like hanging a cane pole in the lake back home," Chrissy admitted.

"I'm from Kansas City," he told her letting the lure drift with the current.

"It's so wonderful the way college brings together people from all over the country," she concluded, hoping she didn't sound too sappy.

"Did you have fun today?" he asked, glancing at her over his shoulder.

"It was wonderful. You're a great guide."

"You're not a bad hiker yourself—" There was

a splash as a trout jumped out of the river to grab the fly.

"You've got one!" Chrissy cried, nearly falling off her rock as she jumped to her feet.

"We don't have it yet. Trout can really put up a fight." He slowly reeled in the line, playing the fish like an expert.

"What can I do?" Chrissy stood at the edge of the water, poised on her toes to get a good view of the struggle. She'd do just about anything to insure she'd be having fried fish instead of a peanut-butter-and-jelly sandwich.

"You can get the net ready. Get it wet," he instructed, his jaw clenched in determination.

She scrambled back to the shore, only to find the net tangled in a snarl of twigs. Muttering under her breath, she hurried to pull the junk out of the netting before she missed all the action.

"Are you coming?" he called out.

She tossed the last twig aside and rushed back to the river's edge. Joe had the fish just two feet from him.

"I need the net now!"

Without giving a single thought to her clothes, she plunged into the freezing water. His hand covered hers on the handle and they netted the big trout together.

"We did it!" she cried.

"You're one of the best camp buddies I've ever had," he told her, handing over the netted fish.

"Hey! Don't get carried away," she warned him as they plodded toward shore.

"What's wrong? Don't you like our finned friend?"

"I just want you to know, I stop once we hit land. I don't clean fish. That's what my brothers are for."

He looked over both shoulders and smiled at her mischievously. "I don't see them anywhere."

"I don't need them. I've got you."

Back on solid ground, Joe put the trout on a stringer and adjusted his waders. He was ready to check his lure and go back to the river when he glanced at Chrissy. "You're soaking wet!"

Chrissy looked down at the water puddling at her feet, her teeth chattering. "Maybe I shouldn't have gone into the water. But how else was I supposed to bring you the net?"

He pulled off his jacket and wrapped it around her shaking shoulders. "We're going to have to settle for just one fish. You need to get back to camp right away to change your clothes. Your stuff can dry by the campfire tonight."

"Even my boots?" she asked, lifting one very heavy foot.

He shook his head, "I've seen people do strange things to get out of cleaning fish. But you're the best."

She hoped he meant that remark in more ways than one. When Joe had joined them on the hike, she hadn't dared hope for anything like what was happening. Tall, dark, handsome, and rugged— Caroline was going to flip when she saw Joe! Behind her back she crossed her fingers, hoping

Joe would stick around long enough for her
cousin to meet him. Otherwise, Caroline
wouldn't believe it when she tried to tell her
about the gorgeous guy she'd met in the un-
sophisticated Climbing Club.

Chapter 10

"What are you girls doing loitering here on a Sunday afternoon?" Will asked.

"Loitering?" Ellis rolled her eyes as if she couldn't believe the insult.

"We're trying to escape the stack of books on our desks back in the dorm," Caroline admitted.

"After just one week of classes?" Will shook his head. "I held out until the second semester of my sophomore year before I started running away from my desk."

"Are you saying we're bad students?" Ellis inquired.

"No way! I'm saying you're both great Music Society members!"

Caroline smiled at Ellis. Their gold-edged invitations to join the society had been hand-delivered to their door Wednesday morning. Since then, life at Colorado University had improved one hundred percent.

"Did you hear about the meeting Tuesday afternoon?" Will asked. "We have to plan a reception or something."

"What time?" Ellis wanted to know.

"Around five."

"Where?"

Will chuckled, but his smile didn't quite reach his cool blue eyes. "I forgot you girls are new. We'll meet in the lobby at the music building. That reminds me. Do you know about the lounge behind the stage? If you're ever looking for someone in the society, check there first."

"What's this? An official meeting taking place without me?" Annette pouted as she joined the group next to the student mailboxes.

"We wouldn't dream of meeting without you," Will vowed.

She smiled and touched the thick braid at the back of her head. "Of of course you wouldn't. A meeting without me wouldn't be very interesting, would it?" There was a commotion at the door, and a sixth sense warned Caroline that something out of the ordinary was about to happen. When she glanced over her shoulder and saw Chrissy walking into the Student Union along with some guy who looked like a lumberjack, she understood her intuition. After two years with Chrissy, she could almost always detect an impending disaster.

"Cara!" Chrissy shouted.

"Who is that girl?" Annette asked. "She looks like a pack mule."

Caroline laughed in spite of herself. Considering the backpack hanging over one of Chrissy's shoulders and the sleeping bag tucked under her other arm, Annette's description had been quite appropriate.

"She's Caroline's cousin," Ellis told the others.

Annette's gaze slipped from Caroline's tasteful earrings, print skirt, and new navy flats to Chrissy's heavy mountain boots. "I don't believe you. That's a terrible joke, Ellis."

"It's true." Both Will and Annette were quiet when Caroline confirmed Ellis's report.

Chrissy said something to her big companion, then both of them started clumping toward the Music Society group. Caroline closed her eyes and wished she'd wake up from the nightmare that was about to happen. She'd known it would be awkward introducing Chrissy to her new friends, but it was going to be impossible with her cousin looking like some kind of nature freak. To make things worse, she had a guy with her who looked like he should have stayed up in the mountains.

"We just got back from the camping trip," Chrissy announced. Will and Annette gave Caroline a wide-eyed look.

"Camping, as a living in a tent?" Annette grimaced as if sleeping out in the open would be nothing short of torture.

Chrissy smiled up at the mountain man, and Caroline knew her friends were going to jump to the wrong conclusion.

"Was this a co-ed trip?" Will inquired in very proper tones.

"There were both boys and girls on the trip," Chrissy answered innocently.

"But we had separate tents," the mountain man added.

"Yeah. I stayed with Nan," Chrissy told her cousin. "Remember my biology partner? The Frisbee player?"

"Frisbee? I thought we were talking about the mountains." Annette shook her head.

"The mountains are unbelievable." Chrissy sighed. "You'll have to come along on one of the trips, Cara. It's impossible to explain how beautiful it was—you'll have to see it for yourself."

Annette giggled and Will stared at the floor.

"I'm not exactly the mountain-climbing type," Caroline said quietly.

"We can take her up sometime, can't we, Joe?"

Chrissy's sappy expression told Caroline her cousin had fallen for the big guy. For Chrissy's sake, she didn't want to be rude. "We can talk about that later. Who's your friend?"

"Joe Thornton. He's another member of the Climbing Club." Chrissy grinned wide enough to show off all her teeth. "Joe, this is my cousin Caroline Kirby."

He shoved a huge hand toward Caroline. "It's nice to meet you, Caroline."

"It's nice to meet you, too . . . Joe."

"I'd be happy to show you the mountains, Caroline," Joe offered.

His broad smile made Caroline wonder if he was being friendly to impress Chrissy. *To each his own*, Caroline thought to herself.

"I've got to unpack," Chrissy said. "Can we talk later?"

"Sure. I'll come over to see you." Caroline wanted to spare Ellis the details of Chrissy's crush. And it would be kinder to spare Chrissy from the comments Ellis would be certain to make about Joe and the mountains.

"Maybe she has a souvenir for you," Annette teased when Chrissy and Joe were barely out of earshot.

"You two are distant cousins, I assume," Will said in his cool, cutting away.

Caroline watched Chrissy and Joe walk toward the doors at the opposite end of the building. It was obvious she was going to have to keep her new friends and Chrissy as far apart as possible.

"I'm so glad you actually came!" Chrissy exclaimed when Caroline stepped into her room at Culver Hall.

"What made you think I wouldn't show up?" Caroline asked.

"You and your friends didn't seem too thrilled to see me today," she said quietly.

"I think you got the wrong idea about my new friends."

"Those weren't the Music Society people, were they?" Chrissy looked quizzically at her cousin. What was happening to Caroline? "You said the Music Society members were the best people on campus."

"They come from very good families," she said, jumping to their defense.

"Well, they have a strange way of showing how well bred they are," Chrissy said, her voice dripping with sarcasm.

"You're not being fair. Annette was just in a bad mood today."

"You don't have to stick up for them." Chrissy stubbornly folded her arms over her chest. "The girl was a snob and the boy was stuffy. How can you tell me you have fun with them?"

Caroline shrugged. "What can I say? They're exactly the kind of people I wanted to meet."

"You actually want to spend time with snobs and bores?" They had only been apart for a few weeks. Could Caroline have changed that much since the month they'd spent together during the summer in New York?

"No. I'm looking for people who have the same priorities as I do." Before Chrissy could say another word about her new friends, Caroline continued, "They aren't snobs and bores. You have the wrong impression of them."

Chrissy held her breath and thought for a moment. "Maybe you're right," she said quickly. "I was so excited about my trip that I wasn't on my best behavior, either. I'll reserve my opinion until I get to know them better."

"Was it really the trip that distracted you?" Caroline teased. "Weren't you really excited about . . . Joe?"

Chrissy's whole body seemed to go limp at the mention of his name. "Isn't he wonderful?" she said dreamily.

"He's quite a guy," Caroline replied, choosing her words carefully.

Chrissy overlooked her cousin's lack of enthusiasm. "This morning when we were packing up our gear, he told me I was a good sport. Do you think that's a good sign? I think it is."

"Are you asking me if he likes you?" Caroline asked. "I really can't say how he feels. . . ."

"But?" Chrissy could tell her cousin had more to say.

"But I can see you've got a gigantic crush on him."

Chrissy felt her cheeks grow warm. Caroline didn't have to make it sound like she was some silly kid in high school. Hadn't they outgrown crushes? She wanted to have a meaningful relationship with Joe. Hiking with him had been fun, but all afternoon she'd been thinking about studying with him, eating dinner with him, going to movies with him—the list was endless.

"You're blushing!" Caroline cried. "I bet you're embarrassed about falling for the first guy you met on campus."

"I'm not embarrassed about Joe in any way," she vowed. "He's great!"

Caroline raised her eyebrows. "I've met a pretty interesting man myself."

"Will?" Chrissy hoped her cousin had better taste than to pick a guy who seemed to think he was too good to acknowledge anyone else's presence. She had to remind herself that she'd promised not to make any judgment on Caroline's new friends until she got to know them better.

"No, not Will," she said patiently. "Robert Winston."

"The guy who caught you when you fell off Elmer Frame?"

"I didn't fall, I was dropped," Caroline corrected. "Anyway, Robert's the graduate assistant who sponsors the Music Society."

"What's so special about him?" Chrissy asked, wondering what Caroline could possibly have in common with a guy who was so much older than herself.

"He's . . . sophisticated. And he was friendlier than some of the others," Caroline explained.

The sparkle in her cousin's eyes made Chrissy curious. "How friendly?"

"He tried to make me feel welcome. I was nervous at the first meeting, and he made me feel comfortable."

Chrissy wasn't sure how to ask the question that had to be asked. "What about Luke?" she blurted out finally.

"I love Luke," said Caroline. "You know that."

She sounded so sure of herself that Chrissy didn't dare question her anymore, but something about the way her cousin talked about Robert Winston was making her uneasy.

"Really, Chrissy. I'm not kidding when I say Luke's still the most important person in my life."

"I believe you, Cara. You don't need to convince me." She only hoped her cousin wouldn't have too hard a time trying to convince herself.

Chapter 11

"Slow down so a mere mortal can keep up with you," Ellis cried as they hurried to the music building Tuesday afternoon.

Caroline slowed her steps. "Sorry."

"Why are you so excited to get to the meeting?" Ellis toyed with her silver pendant. "Do you have the hots for one of the guys? Will? Paul?"

"I'm just anxious to see everyone again," Caroline insisted.

Ellis seemed to believe the explanation. "They are a pretty great group, aren't they?"

Caroline had to agree. Why else would she have butterflies in her stomach as they approached the building?

Robert was standing in the center of the lobby with society members sitting around him on the modular furniture. He winked at Ellis and Caroline when they found seats behind Paul.

Caroline grinned at him. She wondered if he was thinking of the Elmer Frame affair. Maybe by winking he was telling her that it was their secret.

"We were notified that Horton Williams will be performing on campus Saturday evening," Robert announced in his deep voice. "For those of you who are new, the school had arranged for Williams to do a concert here, but he was already booked for the evening. The conflict was resolved suddenly over the weekend, and he will be in this concert hall in four days." He pointed to the doors behind him.

"What does it have to do with us?" Annette asked.

"The head of the music department has asked for our help."

This news was met with almost unanimous groans. However, Caroline thought the concert sounded exciting. She'd accompanied her parents to a Horton Williams concert last spring. He was one of the most impressive young pianists in the country. It was rumored he would have his Carnegie Hall debut before the end of the year.

"I am looking for ushers to hand out programs," Robert said.

Annette waved her hand in the air to Caroline's surprise. Ushering somehow seemed like a job Annette would consider beneath her.

"I'll help. I have the greatest new strapless black dress."

"We'll all be looking forward to seeing it." Robert grinned as he accepted Annette's offer.

"Let's do it," Ellis whispered. "I've got that white dress with the beaded top. And that pale blue dress in your closet would be perfect."

Caroline hadn't imagined that the concert would turn into a fashion show. When she didn't reply, Ellis asked urgently, "Do you want to do it or not?"

"Sure." They both raised their hands.

"Ellis and Caroline." Robert sounded pleased. "I'm happy to see our new members taking an active interest."

"Don't bet on it," Will said. "After their feet get sore on Saturday, they won't be volunteering again."

Robert didn't seem to take the remark seriously.

"Finally, I'd like to find one or two people to help me coordinate the refreshments for the reception." When no one volunteered, he tried to sweeten the request. "I'll do most of the work if someone will at least give me a little moral support."

"Should we?" Caroline whispered to Ellis.

"Help with the food?" She wrinkled her nose. "That's what caterers are for."

Robert locked his hands behind his back and stared at the group. "Maybe I should stand by the door, refusing to let any of you leave until I have my volunteer."

This was ridiculous. Caroline was sure he had

other responsibilities as a teaching assistant, not to mention his own graduate course work. When she raised her hand, she told herself he needed her help, even though the idea of serving food reminded her of the Alpha Thedas. *It has nothing to do with spending time with an interesting man,* she promised herself.

Ellis glared at her, but Robert sighed with relief. "Thank you, Ms. Kirby. You have rescued me."

As the others left, they teased her about falling for Robert Winston's strong-arm tactics. Will assured her she would never volunteer again after the concert.

"What's the big deal about helping with the reception buffet?" she asked when the others had left.

Robert's grin reminded Caroline of a spider inviting a fly into his web. Maybe the others had had good reasons for avoiding this task. "Is there something I should know?"

"Just this." He picked up a folder from a chair and pulled out a scribbled sheet of paper. "Professor Hatch prefers ham slices rolled around melon. Dr. Richards hates ham, but loves chicken wings. Professor Capehart has a thing for tuna finger sandwiches."

Caroline shook her head over the culinary politics. "What do you do? Have a little of everything?"

"It can't be done," he informed her. "If Dr. Richards even sees a hint of ham, he stalks out of the reception. And Hatch is allergic to tuna."

"So why don't we just serve popcorn?" she joked.

Robert smiled at her. "That's an interesting idea. Usually we rotate the menu. After our last concert we had ham rolls. So this time we should serve chicken wings."

"Then it's settled."

"Not quite. Capehart won a Kellerman Fellowship award over the summer, and that gives him some privileges this year."

"Then we should order tuna finger sandwiches."

"We'll risk disappointing Hatch. He might even leave the event."

"He would miss a chance to meet Horton Williams just because tuna gives him hives? I'd be so honored to shake hands with the man that I wouldn't care what I ate."

"You know Williams's work?" Robert seemed pleasantly surprised.

"I heard him in San Francisco last spring," Caroline explained.

"Did he play Chopin that night?" Caroline nodded. "I heard him play in Chicago. It left me breathless."

"How can any one person have that much talent?" she wondered aloud.

"It's a gift," he said with reverence.

"Do you play the piano?" she asked.

"I do, but I'm not pursuing a master's degree in performance. I'm a composer."

She stared at him admiringly. "You write music?"

He nodded. "You're the first person in the society to find that impressive. Thank you."

Caroline didn't know what to say. Anything that came to mind would sound like she was criticizing the other members, and she didn't want to do that behind their backs, since everyone seemed to have accepted her.

The silence became awkward and Robert cleared his throat. "Back to the menu. Do you recommend we go with the tuna to acknowledge Professor Capehart's achievement, and hope Horton Williams is sufficiently impressive to keep Professor Hatch at the reception?"

Caroline nodded. "That's my recommendation."

"Accepted," Robert pronounced. He reached out to shake her hand, and the instant his hand touched hers, Caroline's arm tingled up to her shoulder. She swallowed hard. *This can't be happening,* she told herself. *I'm Luke's girl.* But if that were true, how could she enjoy spending time with Robert Winston so much?

Chrissy leaned on the brick wall and tried not to think about all the homework she should be doing instead of hanging around the music building. But she had promised Caroline she would give her Music Society friends a chance.

When the door opened at last, Chrissy jumped to attention. She blinked twice, hoping she wasn't really seeing what she thought she was seeing. Maybe the late-afternoon sun was playing tricks on her eyes.

"Everything will be fine," Caroline laughed. "Don't worry about Professor Hatch."

The tall, thin man wearing wire glasses gently rested a hand on her cousin's shoulder. *Friendly?* Two nights ago, Caroline had promised that she liked Robert Winston because he was friendly. She said he'd made her feel comfortable at the first Music Society meeting. Well, Chrissy Madden wasn't born yesterday—she could see what was happening! Robert Winston was putting the moves on her cousin!

"Cara!" she called, determined to rescue her cousin before the older man could take advantage of Cara's trust.

"Chrissy?" Caroline shaded her eyes from the sun. "What are you doing here?"

"I came to meet your friends. Remember?"

Caroline nodded. "Robert, I've got to go."

"That's fine." He smiled down at her. "You've been a great help. Thanks."

"What did you do for him?" Chrissy asked when Caroline led her into the music building.

"I'm helping Robert plan the reception for Saturday's concert. There's going to be a classical pianist performing on campus."

"That was nice of you." Chrissy didn't have enough evidence to warn her cousin that Robert Winston might have less than honorable intentions. "Hey, where are we going?"

"There's a private lounge behind the stage. You can always find society members there."

Chrissy bit her tongue before she could say that this lounge seemed like one more example of how stuck-up they were. Why wasn't the music building available to anyone who wanted to be there?

"Caroline! You survived!" someone called out as they entered the lounge.

"Who won? Richards, Hatch, or Capehart?" Will wanted to know.

Caroline laughed. "You've all been through this before!"

"Once," he groaned. "And once was enough."

Caroline sat down in a huge leather chair, and Chrissy perched on the arm of it. Apparently her cousin wasn't going to introduce her, and maybe it was better this way. She could observe the illustrious Music Society without getting involved.

"I read in the *Wall Street Journal* that your dad's company just bought out Star Industries," Will told Paul.

"Yes," said Paul. "Dad's doing okay."

"My Uncle Hank will be in Denver tomorrow night," Annette announced. "Anyone who wants to join us for dinner is welcome."

Chrissy was fascinated by the pocket diaries that popped into sight. Annette's Uncle Hank must be someone awesome like a senator or the president of a major corporation, she decided.

"He is looking for investors, isn't he?" Will

asked before he penciled the meeting into his calendar.

"Of course." Annette ran her hands through her auburn hair.

"You're going to invest in some stocks, Paul?" Ellis asked.

"Don't laugh. Hank has his hand on the pulse of the market," he explained.

Chrissy's mouth fell open. Why were these college kids thinking about stock-market investments? she wondered.

Paul snapped his fingers. "My freshman year, Hank gave me a tip. I ignored it, and he made four million dollars' profit. I kicked myself for not investing in that one, but I was just a freshman at the time and a little nervous."

"I don't want to make that same mistake," Ellis declared.

"My uncle's limo will be waiting outside this building at six-thirty. I'll count you in," Annette said, taking down the names of the interested parties. "Caroline? What about you?"

"Not this time," she said easily.

Not this time? Did that mean her cousin was going to be in the next limo Uncle Hank sent up to campus?

Caroline touched Chrissy's arm. "We've got to be going. But I want to hear all about the dinner in Denver."

"We'll tell you, if you promise not to throw a tantrum when you realize what you missed."

"I promise." Caroline didn't say anything else

until they were safely outside the building. "Did you believe all that?"

Chrissy's heart lightened. Caroline was seeing the truth about her "friends"! "I've never seen anything like it."

"They're actually taking about investing. They're not waiting until they graduate to build their fortunes."

Chrissy stared at her cousin as they walked toward the dorms. Caroline was *impressed* by what she had seen and heard in the private lounge!

"Do you want to know what I thought of them?" Chrissy burst out. "They were talking about their parents' businesses and investments because they have nothing interesting to say about themselves!" Chrissy continued without waiting for her cousin's answer.

"That's not true!"

"No? Do they ever talk about their classes? Do they ever go to class?"

Caroline was quiet for a minute. "I haven't heard them talk about anything that happens on campus."

"You know why? They are too busy pretending they are wheeler-dealers like their parents."

"What's wrong with that? I think their goals are admirable."

"Sure, goals are fine," Chrissy allowed. "But what's wrong with being yourself and acting your own age? We'll be thirty before we know it. Why throw away years of your life by playacting that you're already that old?"

"That's not what they're doing," Caroline insisted.

"Fine." Chrissy could see she wasn't getting anywhere with her cousin. "But if you don't mind, I'll stick with my own friends."

Caroline frowned. "I couldn't have thought of a better solution myself."

Chapter 12

"You're sure you don't mind helping me?" Nan asked, her voice wavering as she and Chrissy waited at their lab station.

"Of course. Didn't you chase that snake away from me last week?" Chrissy wasn't worried about dissecting a rat. She had already done it in biology at Maxwell High.

Professor Kelm delivered a bottled rat to each station and reviewed the procedure before he would let anyone start. When he gave permission for everyone to open their bottles, the burning smell of formaldehyde flooded the room.

"This place smells like our dorm refrigerator," one girl claimed.

"Nothing in the world could smell this bad," the boy next to Chrissy insisted.

"You've never been on a farm," Chrissy guessed.

"Guilty," he admitted. "I'm a city boy."

"Then you'll have to trust me. On a hot summer day, a barn can smell a hundred times worse than this!"

"That does it!" someone else called. "I'm going to get good grades just so I can find a fantastic office job."

"Actually, it's not so bad," Chrissy said.

"Give up, Chrissy. You're not going to change my mind!" the boy persisted.

"You don't know what it's really like."

He took a deep breath of the formaldehyde-filled air and immediately coughed. "I think I have a pretty good idea."

Everyone laughed, and Chrissy couldn't help joining them. They weren't making fun of her, after all. They were just trying to survive a two-hour lab session.

"Will you please do the cutting?" Nan requested when the laughter quieted down.

Chrissy took one look at her partner's pale face. "Sure. You can watch."

She worked quickly and silently, making one big slice and pinning back the skin flaps. Dissection wasn't one of her favorite class assignments, but it clearly didn't bother her as much as it did Nan. Her partner was gripping the counter top so hard that her knuckles were turning white. How could a girl who enjoyed camping in the mountains be terrified of a dead rat?

"We have to identify the organs," she told Nan, who just sat there looking ill. Chrissy set the class handout in front of them and tried to find the heart. Unfortunately, the thing sitting where the heart should be according to the chart didn't look much like a heart. Next she tried to find the stomach, but her luck didn't improve.

"How's it going, ladies?" the teacher inquired as he passed their table.

Knowing Nan was in no condition to speak, Chrissy confessed, "I'm having some problems identifying the organs in my rat."

"Let me have a look," he said, sounding certain he could solve her problem immediately.

He stared at the rat. Then he adjusted his glasses and borrowed Chrissy's stick to gently probe inside the creature. Nan moaned softly and leaned against the counter.

"Class!" he cried. "This is amazing. This rat was pregnant! This is a great chance for you to see how the organs rearrange to accommodate the embryos."

He stepped back to make room for the other students. Before anyone could reach their station, Nan gasped for air and then collapsed into Professor Kelm's arms.

"Ms. Sanderson!"

Chrissy couldn't help giggling at the professor's petrified expression. This man faced bug-infested ecosystems and analyzed dead rats without flinching, but Nan was scaring him half to death.

"Don't worry," Chrissy reassured him. "She just fainted."

"No one ever did that in my class before," he told her.

"Just bring her over to a chair," Chrissy instructed, taking charge. "Put her head between her knees. Someone get a cold towel."

"Should I boil water?" the city boy asked.

Chrissy wondered how he had managed to live eighteen years with so little information. "That's for having babies. Nan fainted. You're making a big deal about nothing."

"What happened?" Nan moaned.

"You see, everybody?" Chrissy said. "She's going to be just fine!"

"Chrissy, it's me!" Caroline called through the closed door.

She heard footsteps inside the room. "We didn't hear you knock. Sorry," Chrissy apologized as she opened the door.

Inside the room the bowl of popcorn made her think they had been partying. "It doesn't look like you guys are working too hard."

"We're just taking a break," Denise explained. "I have three pages of calculus problems to tackle."

"She needed some energy food." Chrissy pointed to the bowl. "Have some."

Caroline pulled Chrissy's desk chair up to the bed and took a handful of popcorn. "Thanks."

"Chrissy was just telling me about the disaster in her biology lab session."

"I heard something happened in the morning lab," Caroline remembered. "Was it in your class?"

"It sure was," her cousin said proudly.

How could she have doubted that Chrissy would be involved if there had been some kind of scene? "What happened?"

"Nan, my partner, has a problem with dissection, to say the least," Chrissy began.

"She didn't lose her breakfast, did she?" The idea of someone throwing up during biology was disgusting.

"Nan didn't do that," Chrissy assured her. Caroline wouldn't put it past someone who camped in the mountains, but she kept the thought to herself and let her cousin continue. "She was really quiet, and then she turned very pale."

"That's when the teacher discovered that the rat Chrissy and Nan were dissecting was pregnant!" Denise added, obviously amused by the story.

"That's gross!" Caroline cried.

"Nan agreed with you," Chrissy said. "She fainted right into Professor Kelm's arms!"

"That's even grosser." Caroline grimaced at the idea of fainting into her professor's arms. He smelled like a petrie dish.

"But you haven't heard the best part." Denise

stuffed a handful of popcorn into her mouth and let Chrissy finish the story.

"It seems like fainting females are Kelm's Achille's heel. He didn't know what to do with Nan hanging in his arms like a rag doll. So I had to take charge," Chrissy announced proudly.

"You did *what*?" Caroline thought there must have been other options, but she knew it never would have occurred to Chrissy to go for help. Her cousin *enjoyed* jumping into the middle of any disaster she could find.

"And she single-handedly saved Nan." Denise made it sound like Chrissy had performed a miracle.

"I hate to break it to you, ladies, but fainting isn't fatal." Caroline rolled her eyes.

"Of course it isn't." Chrissy sounded offended. "I was just doing all I could to help a friend. Do you think Annette or Ellis would do as much for you?"

"I didn't come here to fight about my friends," Caroline said, talking a deep breath to hold on to her patience. "I came because I had a letter from Luke.

"Luke! Did you bring it with you?" Chrissy scooted to the edge of the bed, anxious to read the letter.

"It was pretty personal," Caroline told her. Just thinking about some of things he'd written made her feel all warm inside.

"How does he like the Air Force Academy?"

Chrissy asked. "Or is that information too personal to reveal?"

"Don't be silly," Caroline scolded. "He says the Academy is hard, and he wants me to visit him one of these weekends."

"He'd probably really enjoy some company," Denise said. "My neighbor back home went to the Academy. Freshman year is pretty rough. We might think the Culver Hall Stalker was bad, but that would just be a simple prank at the Academy."

"He didn't sound unhappy . . . ," Caroline began.

"I didn't mean he had to hate it there," Denise hurried to explain. "My neighbor just mentioned how nice it was to see someone from home once in a while to remind him there was a world outside the Academy walls."

"You should go," Chrissy urged.

"I can't go this weekend. I promised to be at the concert."

"Helping Robert Winston is more important than seeing Luke?" Chrissy asked, raising an eyebrow.

"I should be at the reception in case there are any complications," Caroline defended herself. "But more important, I agreed to be one of the ushers."

"I guess you can't walk out on them," Chrissy agreed.

"But I will visit Luke soon," Caroline told her. "I miss him so much."

"I know what you mean. I've been missing Joe," Chrissy confessed.

Caroline swallowed hard when her cousin mentioned her most recent crush. She busied herself picking fuzz balls off her sweater sleeve.

"You didn't see him around today?" Denise asked, not seeming to notice Caroline's distress.

"No, but it's not a problem. He probably has tons of work." Chrissy glanced at the pile of books on her desk. "I have plenty to keep me busy."

Caroline bit her cheek and hoped nothing in her expression would hint that she knew more than she wanted to know about Joe Thornton. He had called her Monday night, but Ellis had taken a message. He had phoned against last night and tried to talk her into meeting him at The Rocky Mountain Club in the Student Union.

What was she supposed to do about the big, ill-mannered guy who insisted she was the prettiest girl he'd ever seen? Even if Chrissy wasn't in love with him, it would be awkward. She didn't like Joe Thornton and she didn't want to be seen with him. Making matters worse, it would destroy Chrissy if she found out that Joe was trying to date her cousin. He certainly hadn't called her because he'd been too busy trying to chase her cousin!

"Earth to Caroline!"

Caroline blinked when she realized her cousin was waving a hand in front of her face. If Chrissy had taken up mind reading, she was deep trouble.

"Can you stay and help us?" Chrissy begged.

"Help you?" What if Chrissy wanted advice about Joe? That guy had her feeling like a rat when she hadn't done anything wrong! If she was smart, she'd avoid her cousin until she had settled things with Joe Thornton.

"Could you help us with our French?" Denise requested. "We have a verbal vocabulary test tomorrow."

"And we really need your help," Chrissy insisted. "Just listen."

"*La mère*," Denise said with a midwestern twang.

"*Le père*." Chrissy sounded like she was talking about a piece of fruit, not someone's father.

They weren't kidding—these girls really did need help. Trying to get her cousin a passing grade was the least she could do to make up for ruining Chrissy's romance. Caroline pushed up her sleeves and leaned forward so they could hear her clearly. "Let's try working on your *r*'s," she began, realizing it was going to be a long night.

Chapter 13

"Over here, Cara!" Joe yelled from a table in the corner of The Rocky Mountain Club.

She ground her teeth, not sure which annoyed her more—that he had drawn attention to her, or that he had used her nickname. She was Cara to family and close friends. He didn't qualify in either category.

"Sit here," he said, patting the part of the bench his muscular frame wasn't covering.

"I prefer a chair," she told him. It was bad enough having to sit opposite him in this dim corner. She certainly wasn't going to snuggle up next to him.

He was on his feet in a second, making a production of pulling out her chair in an effort to be a gentleman. "I've ordered Cokes and onion rings for us."

"That will be fine." If he planned to eat onions, he couldn't be planning to make any moves on her, thank goodness.

He rested his arms on the table and leaned forward. "I'm so glad you came."

Caroline bit her lower lip. She had come to tell him nothing was ever going to happen between them—no matter how hard or how long he tried to start a relationship. Most guys would have gotten the message after she avoided seven phone calls, but Joe Thornton was one of those thick-headed guys who couldn't take a hint.

"I've embarrassed you," he said, misinterpreting her silence. "I'm sorry."

His apology took her by surprise. She hadn't given him credit for having one well-mannered bone in his body. That had been silly. Chrissy must have found something redeeming in the guy if she liked him so much.

"Have you seen Chrissy since the camping trip?" she asked, knowing he'd been avoiding her probably. However, it didn't hurt to bring her name into the conversation and jog his memory.

"What a sport!" he said. "Some freshmen are a real pain on their first trip, but your cousin's a great camper!"

"She thought the mountains were beautiful."

"They are." He raised his eyebrows. "When can we go on a trip up there?"

Caroline shrugged. "I'm not exactly the nature type."

"I know." It didn't seem to bother him in the least. "You wouldn't need hiking boots to go for a drive."

"You're right." Caroline had to smile when she imagined herself wearing Chrissy's clunky boots.

"Let's do it Saturday. I'm sure I can borrow a car. Could you put together a picnic lunch?"

She saw how his enthusiasm could be infectious—to someone who liked him. While she couldn't get used to someone who hollered "Over here, Cara!" for the whole world to hear, Caroline knew she had to do whatever she could to send him back to her cousin.

"I can't do it," she protested.

"No problem. If you can't pack a lunch, we'll grab something from a fast-food place on our way out of town." He grinned. "You're going to love the mountains!"

"I can't go with you," she said quickly before he made any more plans. "I have too many assignments. I can't afford to take off a whole day."

He nodded as if he understood her problem. "Freshman neurosis."

"Excuse me?"

"First-semester freshmen either party non-stop or else they study until they're cross-eyed." He tilted his head to take a good look at her. "You're too pretty to waste away in the library. Let me take you away."

Caroline's blond hair brushed her shoulders

when she shook her head. "I couldn't ask you to do that."

"But I want to," he insisted. "I'll let you study Saturday afternoon, if you'll go to a movie with me Saturday night." Before she could reply, he added, "You owe it to yourself to have a little fun."

She told herself to stop being so polite as the waitress set the onion rings on the table. Joe wasn't going to get her message unless she was more blunt. "I can't."

"Why not?"

"I can't go out with you. Not Saturday afternoon. Not Saturday night. Not—"

"Is there someone else?" he asked. The look in his eyes told her he hated to ask the question.

It was time to tell him about Luke. "I date a guy at the Air Force Academy."

"Someone you just met?" he asked, a spark of hope in his eyes.

"Someone I've cared about for two years," she replied. In truth, they hadn't been together more than a few times during the two years, but it didn't make any difference. She loved him.

He sipped on his Coke. Then he gave her a toothy smile. "Can we see each other as friends?"

"I don't know . . ."

"You don't have to make any decisions now. Just know I'll be here for you if the Air Force guy breaks your heart." He reached across the table for her hand. "In fact, I'll be waiting."

Caroline dropped her hand into her lap, trying

hard not to take his offer as a threat. She didn't want him hanging around, waiting for Luke to dump her. He was supposed to like Chrissy!

"My cousin could use a friend, too," Caroline said, although she knew Chrissy would kill her if she ever found out about a matchmaking attempt.

"Chrissy's a great kid," he said, emphasizing the last word and making his feelings for Chrissy clear.

"There's more to her than meets the eye," Caroline hinted.

"Maybe. But she reminds me of my little sister."

Caroline frowned. There was nothing she could do for her cousin. If she reminded Joe Thornton of his kid sister, there didn't seem to be much hope.

Caroline tried to melt into a crowd of students when she saw Chrissy coming in her direction the next morning, but it was too late.

"Have you seen Joe?" Chrissy asked.

"No." Caroline swallowed hard. "Why are you asking me?"

"Just because you know what he looks like," she said.

Caroline felt like wiping her brow and heaving a huge sigh of relief. Chrissy didn't know about last night—yet. Her cousin was smart enough to suspect something, so Caroline tried to act as normal as possible.

"I've been in my room, or at least in the dorm,

every night this week," Chrissy reported. "He hasn't called. I never see him in the dining hall, but I'm sure he eats."

Caroline thought of Joe wolfing down the whole basket of onion rings after she told him about Luke. "I'm sure he does, too," she agreed.

"Well, I think it's time for me to take things into my own hands," Chrissy announced.

"What are you going to do?" Caroline had visions of her cousin marching into one of Joe's classes and dragging him into the hall for a heart-to-heart.

"I'm going to quit waiting for him to find me. I don't have any afternoon classes today. Joe's going to be my project," she declared. "I'll find him somewhere."

Caroline smiled in spite of the hopelessness of Chrissy's plan. Her cousin could be more determined than any other person on earth. She almost felt sorry for Joe, knowing Chrissy was going to track him down.

"You think it's a good idea?" Chrissy asked.

Caroline couldn't be responsible for misleading her cousin. On the other hand, she couldn't tell Chrissy not to go through with her plan without offering some explanation.

Chrissy smiled, apparently taking her cousin's silence as consent. "I'm glad you agree. Enough about me. What did you do last night?"

Alarmed, Caroline stared at her cousin.

"Hey, don't worry. I'm not going to tell your

parents if you skipped studying for one night," Chrissy teased.

She ran a shaky hand through her bangs. "Thanks. I just couldn't face the books, so I hung around the dorm," she lied.

"Are you sure you're okay?" Chrissy asked. "You look distracted."

"Don't worry about me," Caroline said, desperately trying to think of some way to explain her nerves. "It's been a stressful week. I haven't been the same since I nearly fell off Elmer Frame."

"And I haven't been the same since I got to know Joe," Chrissy confided. "That's why I've got to find him!"

Chapter 14

Where could he be? Chrissy asked herself, still looking for Joe an hour after dinner. She was beginning to think Joe Thornton didn't really go to Colorado University. Maybe he was a non-student who liked to camp. Maybe he had just been a figment of her imagination.

Twice she had searched all the classroom buildings. After she learned he lived in Fowler Hall, she'd hung around the front door for most of the afternoon. She figured he'd come back to the dorm after his last class, but he never did.

Chrissy was almost back to Culver Hall when she had an idea. Denise was meeting some people from her sociology class to discuss a project, and Chrissy didn't feel much like being alone. With any luck, Ellis would be out for the evening and she and Caroline could settle down to some popcorn and conversation. She desperately needed someone to tell her Joe wasn't avoiding her, and that everything would work out all right.

It was a short walk to Fielding Hall. Chrissy almost didn't stop in the lobby since Caroline's room was right down the hall. But something told her she should check around in case Caroline had stopped to talk with some friends.

She wished she hadn't listened to that little voice when she found Caroline and Joe in the lobby, standing so close together that she almost didn't notice her cousin at first. Her back was against the wall and Joe was leaning so close that it seemed as if Caroline might suffocate. At that moment, Chrissy couldn't think of a better end for her cheating lying cousin.

Now she knew why Joe hadn't called her—he'd been too busy with her very own cousin! How had it started? When? Had Caroline decided to steal him the minute she saw him in the Student Union last Sunday? Had she been secretly seeing him ever since then?

Chrissy struggled to catch her breath. How could her cousin do such a mean thing when Caroline knew how she felt about Joe? She want to yell at both of them, but she felt too paralyzed by shock.

However, she knew if she stayed a second longer, she'd find her voice and make a scene she'd probably regret for a long, long time. She ducked her head and hurried out the door.

Outside, she realized she had no place to go. And the last thing she wanted to do was go back to her empty room and feel sorry for herself.

Besides, Caroline had to pay for what she'd done. Since she couldn't challenge her cousin to a duel, she was going to confront Caroline verbally. No one could hurt Chrissy Madden and get away with it!

Chrissy shielded her face from view when she went back through the Fielding Hall lobby. Now that she was thinking more clearly, she knew she didn't want to face both of them. She had nothing to say to fickle Joe Thornton; her business was with her cousin. She would wait in Caroline's room until she could deal with her cousin alone.

"What do *you* want?" Ellis asked rudely when Chrissy pushed open the door to room 136.

"I want to wait for Cara. Alone."

Ellis gasped dramatically. "Excuse me? Are you asking me to leave my own room?"

"Yes."

Ellis stared at Chrissy. "Hey, is something wrong? You look terrible." She wrinkled her nose as if gazing at Chrissy was distasteful.

"My life is ruined," Chrissy muttered, trying to make herself comfortable on Caroline's bed. She didn't think twice about getting her dirty shoes on her cousin's blue satin quilt.

"Did someone die?" Ellis's dark eyes grew large. "Can I get you a glass of water or something?"

"No. I just want to be left alone. What I have to say to Cara is private."

Ellis scrambled to find her shoes and grab her purse. "I was on my way out, anyway. Just tell Cara I'm at the Music Society lounge in case she needs me later."

Chrissy smiled, feeling a strange sense of anticipation about the brawl she was about to stage. She wondered what her cousin's friends in the Music Society would say about one of their members double-crossing her own family?

She closed her eyes to let her anger simmer until Caroline returned. There was no sense letting off all her steam now, saving nothing for her cousin's return. At the first sound of the doorknob moving, Chrissy sat up abruptly, having reached the boiling point despite her efforts to remain calm.

Caroline walked in and blinked at the light. Apparently she had expected the room to be dark and empty. Chrissy decided to catch her by surprise.

"How could you?" she screeched, jumping to her feet.

"How could I what?" Caroline asked, stepping backward in surprise. Chrissy figured her cousin was buying time. She was trying to think of a way to talk herself out of this mess.

"Of all the men on this campus, how could you steal the one guy you knew I liked?" Chrissy glared down her cousin, refusing to look away.

Caroline quickly shut the door to spare the

entire first floor from having to hear their fight. "Steal? Joe?"

"Don't waste your time playing innocent. I saw you with him downstairs, and you looked *very* involved. How long has it been going on?" she examined.

"I don't like Joe," Caroline protested. "You've got it all wrong, Chrissy."

"You always let boys you don't like nuzzle your neck?"

Caroline narrowed her eyes. "He wasn't nuzzling."

"Oh?" Chrissy said, on the verge of exploding, "What would you call what he was doing? Are you trying to say that I imagined the whole thing?"

"He was trying to convince me to go to the football game with him next Saturday afternoon," she said flatly.

Stunned by the pain, Chrissy collapsed on the bed. She thought it would be therapeutic to hear Caroline admit she'd been trying to steal Joe, but she'd been wrong. She could actually imagine him asking her cousin for a date. His brown eyes would be sparkling as he explained what fun they'd have at the game. And after he invited her, he would flash her one of his heart-melting smiles.

Her heart ached as if it had been pierced with a knife. A knife clutched in her cousin's hand.

"I was telling him I wouldn't go," Caroline tried

to explain. "Every time he asks me out I refuse him."

"How many times have there been?" Chrissy couldn't stop herself from asking although it hurt.

"It doesn't matter," she mumbled. "I just want to make it clear that I always turn him down."

Chrissy's voice was strong and clear. "Why?"

Caroline looked at the floor. "I don't like him the way you do."

Chrissy pressed her hands to her cheeks, unable to accept Caroline's words as the truth. "You don't mind cuddling with him, but he's not good enough to be your date? Are you limiting yourself to guys in the Music Society now?"

"Chrissy! You can't say these things! You know I love Luke."

She could only laugh. "That's such a sad excuse."

"Luke is no excuse!"

"Yeah? Then why do you blush around Robert Winston," Chrissy announced.

Caroline sighed heavily as though the whole conversation was too boring for words. "Why are you dragging him into this mess?"

"Because if you're already cheating on Luke with the music department's graduate assistant, why shouldn't you add Joe Thornton to your list of conquests?" Once Chrissy got started, she couldn't stop. "Robert *and* Joe can be your boyfriends at C.U.—Luke would never know the difference!"

Caroline clenched and unclenched her hands at

her side, struggling to stay in control. Very slowly, she said, "I think you'd better leave, Chrissy. Right now."

Chrissy spun around and rested her hand on the doorknob. "College is really changing you, Caroline Kirby."

"I'm not going to listen to any more of—"

"Don't worry," Chrissy interrupted. "You won't have to listen to me again. I won't be back."

"The concert was simply breathtaking," Dr. Richards exclaimed.

"It really was wonderful," Caroline agreed, smiling at the head of the music department. "Horton Williams is amazing."

"Yes, he is." Like Robert, he seemed very happy to find a student who really appreciated music.

Caroline adjusted the thin straps on her shoulders. Ellis had been right about her pale blue dress—it was perfect for the evening. "Uh, Dr. Richards. Have you seen Robert Winston?"

The man straightened his glasses. "Robert?"

"Yes. I'm supposed to be helping him with the refreshments, and he seems to have disappeared."

"Have you checked the hall? That's where the caterers leave the food."

"Thank you." she said as she turned to leave.

She was halfway across the room when Ellis caught up with her. "Where have you been? Will was looking for you."

"I have food duty." She gave Ellis a quick smile that falsely hinted she was sorry she couldn't stick around and chat.

"We could use a few more vegetable sticks to go with the dip," Ellis informed her.

"I'll tell Robert," she said vaguely.

"Why don't you let Robert do all the work?" Ellis suggested. "You should mingle."

"I'll get back to you as soon as I can." Caroline promised slipping away from Ellis quickly before her roommate could think of anything else to detain her.

She easily found the door behind the buffet table. "Robert?" she called out as she entered the room.

"There you are, Caroline." His warm smile made her giggle.

He sounded happy to see her, but not desperate. She assumed everything must be going according to plan. "Do you need any help?"

Robert pushed his hair off his forehead in the way that she found so endearing. "Technically, I have things under control, but I'd appreciate your company."

"It's the least I can do for the man who's doing such a fine job of keeping fresh tuna finger sandwiches on the buffet table," she told him, leaning against a cart.

He reached around her to rearrange two bowls on the cart—two bowls that didn't need moving in Caroline's opinion. As he pulled back, they were suddenly eye to eye. She licked her dry lips and tried to smile, casually.

Robert cleared his throat and stood up straight. "You've really made this reception more interesting than it would have been otherwise. I usually dread choosing the menu, and it's even harder listening to the professors complain about the food."

"I hope I helped a bit."

He winked at her. "You helped a lot. Actually, I was looking forward to tonight because you would be here, and we could spend some time together."

Caroline sighed. Somewhere in the back of her mind, Chrissy's accusation echoed softly. Silently, she insisted to herself that her cousin was wrong. Deep in her heart, she knew Luke was the man for her. But Robert was so charming. What was wrong with enjoying a little time with him? *After all, I came to college to meet new people,* she thought.

"A penny for your thoughts," Robert said softly.

Caroline shook her head, sending Chrissy's harsh woods back to a hidden corner of her brain. "A penny? Haven't you heard of inflation?"

Robert turned out his pants pockets. "And haven't you heard that graduate assistants are notoriously poor?"

Caroline doubted it was true in his case—he had an MG, an apartment, and nice clothes.

"Would you join me on the lawn for dessert after the party breaks up? I picked up a little treat for us." He pointed to a boxed chocolate mousse pie on the cart's lower shelf.

"You bought that for us?" Caroline wasn't sure she believed him.

"I know it was presumptuous he confessed. "But I was passing La Maison Rouge today, and I couldn't help myself. I hope you don't mind."

"How could I mind? I'd love to, but . . ." She thought quickly. "Grass stain would never come out of my skirt."

"I've got a blanket in my car," he volunteered.

"A blanket? Are you a Boy Scout or something?" In spite of herself, Caroline was charmed that he had taken her excuse seriously.

"I have a stadium blanket in the car," he explained. "I go to a lot of the football games."

"I'm sorry. That was really rude of me to say that," she apologized feeling her cheeks begin to color.

"You're blushing! I love it!"

"Stop," she pleaded. Her face was growing hotter.

Gently he touched her red cheek. "You're a special woman, Caroline Kirby. Do you have any idea how special you are?"

Her throat went dry. No matter how hard she tried to swallow, she couldn't do it. Part of her wanted to believe she was special to him. But the other part warned her to leave or else she wouldn't be able to live with her conscience tomorrow morning.

"I'm just me." She shrugged her shoulders, trying not to feel guilty about Luke.

"I'm so glad you are."

A dozen responses ran through Caroline's mind. She could tell him about Luke. Or, she could throw herself in his arms.

"Thanks," she said finally, "I'm looking forward to eating that pie. Chocolate is my favorite."

Chapter 15

"I don't want to be here," Chrissy whispered to Nan when they reached the room on the second floor of the science building.

"You have just as much right to be here as he does," Nan told her firmly.

Chrissy sighed. "I just don't know—it might be easier if I drop out of the club. I can't possibly face him."

"Did you like hiking and camping?" Nan asked impatiently.

"Yes." And she had liked doing it with Joe.

"Then you can't give up all the fun trips in the future just because one guy in the Climbing Club is a jerk!"

"You know Joe's not a jerk," Chrissy protested. "He's your brother's friend."

"I think he was a jerk to lead you on that weekend," Nan said indignantly.

"He didn't lead me on," Chrissy argued, still standing outside the classroom door. "He was a nice guy who fell under my cousin's spell. My mistake was introducing him to her in the first place."

"Are you two joining us today?" Frank asked on his way into the room.

"Are we?" Nan asked Chrissy.

"Why not?" Chrissy led Nan to two desks at the back of the room. It would be easier to stare at the back of Joe's head than to wonder all through the meeting if he was looking at her.

Five minutes later, she had to admit it was a good theory that didn't work. Just being in the same room with Joe made her uncomfortable.

Everyone seemed to have had a good time on the trip. Frank asked if there was any interest in another trip before the winter snows came to the mountains. When Joe raised his hand, Chrissy sat on hers. Nan glared at her.

"I have tons of class work," she whispered.

"Baloney," her friend shot back.

Chrissy slipped a blank piece of paper out of her folder and scribbled, *Watch it, Sanderson. What if I won't help you with the next dissection project?*

Nan turned pale just reading the note.

The meeting didn't last long. As soon as it was adjourned, Chrissy realized there had been one more error in her plan. Sitting at the back of the room, they couldn't escape quickly—and Joe seemed to be waiting to talk to her.

"If I had a fairy godmother, I'd wish myself out of this room right now," Chrissy whispered to her partner.

"I won't abandon you," her friend said, trying to help.

Chrissy's feet froze to the floor when Joe came toward them. He gave her an innocent smile. "How are you, Chrissy?" he asked calmly, as if the world hadn't fallen apart.

"I've been better." She glared at him. He had a lot of nerve to expect her to be friendly.

"Hey, what happened to the happy camper?" When she didn't crack a smile, he asked, "Is something going on here?"

She stood in silence, refusing to make it easy for him.

He glanced at Nan. "I think I need to talk to Chrissy alone."

Chrissy saw concern in her friend's eyes. "I'll be okay," she told Nan, although she wasn't sure she believed it herself.

When Nan stepped into the hall, Joe took a step toward Chrissy, and she immediately took a step backward. She couldn't afford to let him get close enough to make her lower her defenses.

"What's wrong? I thought we had fun on the trip."

"I'm sure you've talked to Cara," she said stiffly. "You must know what's bothering me." It hurt

Chrissy to talk about her cousin, but she wasn't in any mood to play games with Joe.

He though for a moment. "I don't think I've talked to her since last Friday."

That's a surprise. Chrissy had figured her cousin would run to him and cry on his shoulder after their fight. Of course, she might have turned to Robert.

"But she did say something that made me wonder if there was a misunderstanding between you and I," he continued.

"A misunderstanding?" It was one way to describe what had gone down in the last week.

"What did you think . . . happened between us in the mountains?" he ventured.

"I thought you liked me," she said bluntly.

"I do like you—as a friend," he told her.

The old "let's be friends" routine wasn't going to satisfy her. "I liked you more than that."

He actually squirmed. "I was afraid that was the problem."

Afraid? Problem? Chrissy was getting the impression she should apologize for ever crossing Joe Thornton's path. "I didn't realize I was such a nuisance."

Joe stamped his foot, his face a map of frustration. "I'm doing this all wrong."

"That's a distinct possibility," Chrissy told him, not letting him off the hook.

"Look, Chrissy. You're a great camping buddy. I wouldn't mind hiking with you again. It was fun."

"But you'd like to limit it to hiking," she guessed.

He nodded his head sadly. "I'm sorry you got the wrong idea. You're a great kid, Chrissy."

"Thanks," she croaked. "I've got to go."

She had to get away from him in the next ten seconds before she burst into tears. At last she understood what had happened on the mountain. He hadn't taken advantage of her or even tried to mislead her. She had simply read all the signals wrong. *Just because we got along well on the trails doesn't mean there's romance ahead for us,* Chrissy thought bitterly.

"Are you going to be all right?" Nan put an arm around Chrissy's shoulder as soon as she came out of the room.

"I'll be fine. I made a dumb freshman mistake," she told her friend.

"We're going to be pretty smart by the time we get out of this place," Nan said.

"What do you mean?"

"Let's look at the Joe Thornton disaster this way," Nan proposed. "This is one mistake you'll never make again in your life."

Chrissy sniffed and tried to smile at her friend. "I sure hope you're right."

Chrissy slammed her French book closed. "I can't stand it!"

"*Le français* is too hard?" Denise asked. "I haven't looked at the assignment yet."

"I don't understand any of it," Chrissy complained. "All this French stuff reminds me of you-know-who."

"The cousin whose name shall never be mentioned again?" Denise guessed.

"That's right." She pushed her book away. "Let's get out of here."

Denise set aside her calculus notes. "Good idea. I feel like my math book has become a permanent part of my body. Where do you want to go?"

"What about The Rocky Mountain Club?"

"Are you hungry?"

"I wasn't exactly thinking about eating," Chrissy admitted. "How would you feel about looking for men?"

Denise let her head drop on her desk. "I'd love it. I haven't met a guy yet who doesn't look or act like a reject from *Animal House*."

"Consider yourself lucky. I met Mr. Perfect. And I made the mistake of letting him think of me as a good sport when he was looking for someone cute, and feminine."

"He didn't deserve you if he was too blind to see what a good person you are," Denise declared.

Chrissy laughed. "Keep talking. Maybe I'll believe you one of these days.

"What should we wear for man-hunting?" Denise got up from her desk and looked at the ketchup stain on her jeans. "I guess I should change.

"I'm going to wear jeans and that sweater with

buttons at the neck. I think I'll leave the top three undone."

"You're serious tonight!" Denise exclaimed. "I don't have a button-necked sweater. The best I can do is push up my sweat-shirt sleeves."

"I just hope the sight of your bare arms doesn't make the guys crazy," Chrissy teased. It felt good being with Denise, and Nan had been a true friend that afternoon. Who needed Miss What's-her-name from California?

Forty-five minutes later they had eaten enough popcorn to keep a small farm in business. Chrissy looked at her buddy across the table. "Where are the men?"

"I don't know," she admitted. "I can't push my sleeves up much higher without cutting off my circulation."

"I wouldn't want you to hurt yourself. Men aren't worth it," Chrissy mumbled.

"There's one." Denise covertly pointed to a short guy leaving the counter with a hot dog in hand.

"He's not—" Chrissy began.

"But he's alive and breathing," Denise remarked. "How desperate are we?"

Before Chrissy could answer, the male in question sat down at a table with three other guys.

Denise nodded at the table. " That's our biggest problem. They all sit together."

"How much longer do you want to sit here and watch guys ignore us?" Chrissy asked.

Denise shoved her sleeves down to her wrists.

"I can't take it much longer. There's a limit to how many times a person can be rejected."

"Let's go then before one more guy has a chance to snub us."

On the way back to the dorms, Chrissy began to feel really outraged by their failure to improve their social situation. "The more I think about it the madder I get," she told Denise.

"You don't need to be mad at the guys at The Rocky Mountain Club. Tuesday night isn't exactly a great pickup night."

"I'm not thinking about them." Chrissy shook her head. "If a certain relative of mine who shall remain nameless had kept her nose out of my life, I wouldn't have had to sit in that booth tonight at all."

"Are you saying you'd be with Joe?" Denise paused for a moment. "I don't mean to be rude, but I thought he'd explained he only wanted to be friends, even during the camping trip."

Chrissy shook her head. "If he hadn't seen *her*, I think he might have called me about once a week to grab a Coke or whatever. Over time, I think I would have grown on him."

"Like mold?" Denise asked in an attempt to lighten up Chrissy's mood.

Chrissy stuffed her hands in her pockets. "I'm not making myself clear. I think Joe could have liked me if he'd gotten to know me better. But we never had a chance because my traitorous relative swept him off his feet before he knew what was happening to him."

"It's possible," Denise said softly.

"And you know what's the worst thing about it all?"

Denise shook her head. "It's all so rotten."

No matter how many bad things were happening, Chrissy could identify what seemed cruelest to her at the moment. "We're going back to the dorm to study. While I'm spending one more night with my books, my unnamed relative has three guys in love with her!"

"Look at it this way. Who do you think will have better midterm grades?" Denise asked.

"I will. And you-know-who will fail her classes and drop out of school." But Chrissy knew it wouldn't happen because she'd lived two years with the person in question. Her boy-crazed relative was a good student; she wouldn't flunk her classes. *Still, it doesn't hurt to dream,* Chrissy thought viciously, giving a rock a good, solid kick.

Chapter 16

"What about your boyfriend at the Air Force Academy?" Ellis asked.

"What about him?" Caroline fussed with her cowl neckline and wished her roommate wouldn't talk about Luke.

"What if he calls? What should I tell him?" she persisted.

"He won't call." She'd gotten two letters from Luke, but no calls. Caroline assumed he was terribly busy.

"But what—"

Caroline spun around to face her roommate. "Ellis, if you want to know about my date with Robert, just ask me."

"Fine." Ellis tucked her feet beneath her. "How

can you go out with Robert when you already have a boyfriend?"

"I'd accept an invitation from the biggest nerd on campus if he had tickets to the touring production of *Cats*," she said, voicing the argument she'd used herself ever since Robert had presented her with the two tickets.

"It had nothing to do with Robert being your date?"

"The play was sold out months before I ever got to town. How else could I ever hope to see the play?"

"You didn't answer my question." Ellis began drumming her nails on a book, one Caroline figured her roommate had never opened. "I asked you how much Robert had to do with your decision to cheat on Luke, a boy who could be fighting for our country one day."

"Knock it off." Caroline said, though she couldn't help laughing when Ellis got dramatic. "I'm not cheating on Luke. I'm simply going to a play."

"With one of the hottest dates on campus," Ellis remarked.

Caroline dropped her shoe. "Really? Robert?"

"At least among the female members of the Music Society. I don't mean they want to marry him or anything. But I know a few who would kill for a date with him."

Right now Caroline didn't want to think about Robert's sophistication, or how flattered she'd been when he'd invited her to the play. Those were precisely the kind of thoughts that were guaranteed to make her feel guilty, and there was absolutely no reason for her to feel that way. Sitting next to Robert in a huge, dark theater wasn't going to make her love Luke any less.

I've got to keep busy while I'm not with Luke, she told herself. *Otherwise, it's going to be a very long four years.*

"This is a great place," she told Robert as the maître d' of The Hollows escorted them to a table near the massive stone fireplace.

"You should see it in daylight." He pointed toward the expanse of windows across the room. "It's a western view. All you see is mountains."

Robert's remark made Caroline feel subdued. The mountains made her think of Chrissy and Joe.

"The specialty here is prime rib," he told her.

"I don't think I could eat an entire entrée."

He adjusted his wire-rimmed glasses on the bridge of his nose. "Did you eat in the dining hall?"

"I grabbed something earlier." When he looked disappointed, she hurried to add, "I didn't know you had dinner plans."

"Would I take a beautiful woman into Denver for a play and not stop at The Hollows?"

Honestly, Caroline hadn't had any idea what to expect. She smiled at him. "How should I know? I'm new around here."

He ordered the beef for himself and she chose

a chef's salad. After the waiter took their order, Robert sat back in his chair. "Did you enjoy the play?"

"It was wonderful. I was swept away by the story, and the music was fantastic."

He reached out for her hand. "That's why I invited you, Cara. I could barely believe my luck when I met you, someone who can appreciate good theater and music with me."

"Thank you." The compliment washed over Caroline.

"You're sparkling," he said.

"*Pardon*?" she asked with a French accent.

"I'm referring to your dress," he explained. "It shimmered when the house lights came up in the theater, and now it's catching the light from the chandelier."

"Thank you," she said once again. Caroline had chosen the soft sweater dress because it gave her confidence. She hadn't realized the silver threads woven into the peach-colored knit would make her sparkle.

"You said your father is a music critic in San Francisco?"

"Yes." She took her hand back to brush a few stray hairs out of her face.

"What kind of music does he like?"

"Mostly classical—I feel like I was born at the symphony and the opera. But I've seen him enjoy an experimental piece once in a while." It was much easier talking about her father than accepting compliments from Robert.

"And you?" he asked. "What's your kind of music?"

"I appreciate fine music like Horton Williams and symphony orchestras. But I can't live a whole day without listening to KLLM." He smiled when she mentioned the hot local rock station.

"Sounds healthy," he remarked.

"What kind of music do you write?" She guessed he was composing a piece for strings, or maybe for a wind quintet.

He looked slightly embarrassed when he admitted, " My personal goal is to be the next Stephen Sondheim."

Caroline was delighted when he mentioned the popular composer of *A Little Night Music*. "You want to create the next mega-hit musical for Broadway?"

"I wouldn't mind."

His crooked grin showed Caroline a new side of him. He was more than a sophisticated guy with all the right moves. Robert Winston had dreams, and he wasn't afraid to share them.

"Are you working on anything now?" she asked excitedly.

"I've sent a few tapes of my work to friends of friends in Los Angeles. I'd be happy to score a film or even a television movie."

"You'll have to let me know when your music hits the stage or screen" she told him. "I'll have my father mention you in his column."

He grimaced. "Only if you can promise he'll be kind."

Through dinner they chatted easily about life at Colorado University. Robert told dozens of amusing stories. Yet in spite of herself, Caroline yawned as they walked to his car.

"Sorry. It's not the company. I've had a long week."

"Apology accepted." He helped her into the car.

"We talked about me most of the night. Tell me about you," he said as they pulled out of the parking lot.

"What would you like to know?" she asked sleepily.

"Everything," he said.

His quick answer made her chuckle. "That could take quite a while."

"Why don't you start with the present? What's your major?"

"French literature," she said into the darkness.

He whistled. "That's ambitious—I haven't met too many French-literature majors. What classes do you take?"

"This semester I'm taking art history, European history before 1600, a French novels class ... and biology."

"Good old biology," he said with a grin. "A girl in my class lost her lunch during a lab session."

"Someone fainted in ... my cousin's class." *Why did I say that?* She'd promised herself not to let Chrissy interfere with her evening. "Why do they make us take dumb science classes anyway? I don't need to know about rats to speak or read

French. When's the last time you needed to know about biology to write music?"

Robert shrugged.

"So why is there a science requirement?"

He drove the car onto campus. "It's my theory that the regents do it so they can still feel like they're in control around here."

"That makes as much sense as anything else," Caroline told him. "Guess I'm stuck with the class."

"It sounds to me as if you need your biology class—at least it gets you out of the library. With history and literature classes, I bet you read all the time."

"Sometimes it seems like that's all I do."

"Cara, you're too pretty to spend all your time studying. I'd like to show you around Boulder and Denver."

As long as he didn't offer to drive her into the mountains, Caroline could listen to him talk. She wasn't being disloyal to Luke by having interesting conversations with a graduate student.

He parked the MG in the "no parking" zone in front of Fielding Hall. She waited while he hopped out his door and came around to her side. Robert didn't just open her door; he took her hand and helped her out of the car.

Caroline was impressed when he walked her up the steps to the front door. He was truly a gentleman. When he took her hand and led her to one side of the door, she followed willingly.

"Thank you for a most enjoyable evening," he said softly.

"I should be thanking you," she told him, fascinated by the intense look in his eyes. "I had a wonderful time."

He pulled her closer to him. "I'd like to do it again sometime."

"I don't—"

Before she could try to make some excuse or actually tell him about Luke, she felt his lips pressing against hers. His kiss was warm and inviting, and Caroline's arms slipped around his neck before she knew what she was doing.

Gently he lifted her hands away from him, and Caroline realized she had made a mistake. "I'm sorry," she whispered.

He dropped a quick kiss on the tip of her nose. "Don't be. I just don't want you to think you owe me anything. We both had a good time tonight, and that's enough for me."

Confusion flooded Caroline's brain. She hadn't felt like she owed him a kiss in exchange for their evening together! To be honest, she hadn't been thinking of anything except how nice it felt to be kissing him. *What about Luke*? her conscience screamed. She looked up at Robert. "I've got to go."

He was too nice to ask why she was leaving him so abruptly. Instead, he kissed her hand and then backed down the steps. "I'll see you soon."

"Yes, soon . . ."

Caroline leaned against the brick building, not

caring if the stones snagged her dress. How could she have had such a good time with someone who wasn't Luke? How could it have been so nice to kiss someone who wasn't Luke? She covered her mouth with her hands, totally confused about the evening.

Robert Winston and Luke were nothing at all alike. Robert was smooth and mature. Luke was . . . well, he was just lovable Luke. Was she willing to risk her relationship with Luke for a sophisticated man who flattered her and made her feel incredibly special? Caroline was horrified when she realized she couldn't answer that question.

She wiped a single tear from her cheek and opened the heavy front door to the dorm. Caught up in her own problems, she didn't notice the huge man leaning against the wall.

"Hey, Cara!" Joe called, springing toward her. "I've got great news."

She looked at Joe, asking herself what she had done to deserve him. The only idea she wanted to hear about was how he was going to leave her alone.

"*Rambo Two* is coming to campus this weekend."

"Oh," she said flatly.

"You don't like Rambo movies," he immediately assumed.

"No." Caroline wished with all her heart he would disappear in a puff of smoke. She had some serious thinking to do.

Joe nodded. "Okay. I'll think of something else we can do this weekend."

"Uh, Joe," she said. "I thought we were just friends."

"We are." He flashed her a toothy smile. "I was thinking you must be getting pretty lonely with your boyfriend in Fort Collins. I'm just trying to help out a friend."

"Thanks, but I won't need any help this weekend."

"All right. But promise you'll call if you need me," he requested before he left.

"Fine. I promise." It wasn't exactly a lie, she told herself. She knew she wouldn't be calling him, because she couldn't think of any situation in which she might need him.

"Good night," he called from the door, "and sweet dreams."

Caroline rolled her eyes, hoping no one had heard him. There wasn't a chance in the world that she would have sweet dreams tonight. In fact, she wasn't sure she could even fall asleep before morning.

Back in her room, Caroline realized she desperately needed a friend to talk to. Ellis was gone, but that was all right. Her roommate was much too interested in Robert to give her any trustworthy advice. Besides, Ellis probably wouldn't see anything wrong with a girl dating several men. What she really wanted to do was talk to Chrissy, but that was impossible.

Her eyes caught Luke's last letter, half-tucked

under a book on her desk. Every other time she'd felt lonely or homesick it had helped to curl up on her bed and write to him. Although she could think of nothing else besides Robert and Joe and the mess she was making of her first semester, she reached for her stationery.

She plumped up her pillow and balanced the stationery box on her crossed legs. For a second, she chewed on the cap to her felt-tipped pen. Then she wrote, *Dear Luke*.

Trying to think of something else to write, she began to cry. If she loved Luke, why was everything so hard? Two tears rolled down her cheeks and plopped on the paper. With a sad heart, she watched Luke's name dissolve and smear across the page. She hoped it wasn't some kind of awful omen.

Chapter 17

Until now, Caroline had never considered Thursday her lucky day, but she couldn't help thinking things were looking up for her. She'd gotten a letter from Luke and an A on her French-literature test. When she read Luke's sweet words, things seemed so simple. She would visit him soon, and all doubts would be put to rest.

Feeling too ecstatic to study, she decided to skip viewing art slides at Buttler Library and headed for the music-department lounge. She deserved a chance to relax and have fun with her friends.

She breezed through the lobby where they usually held Music Society business meetings. There was a smile on her face as she came around the back of the stage. The lounge door was open, and the sounds of several people having a conversation carried into the hall.

"But, Ellis, what's going on between Caroline and Robert Winston?"

Caroline paused, curious to hear what they had to say about Robert. If she charged in there right now, she'd never hear what they really thought of him.

"What do you think?" Ellis responded.

"Cara can't be intending to use him for a grade. She's not in any of his classes."

They were talking about her! And from the tone of Annette's voice, they weren't very happy about her friendship with Robert.

"I don't think she has any ulterior motives," Ellis told the other girls. "She just likes him."

"Who wouldn't?"

They all agreed that they'd accept a date with Robert, if he would only ask them. "That's the problem," someone said. "He's never paid any attention to a student or a society member before."

"What's she got that we don't have?" one girl whined. "My daddy could buy him his own band."

"It's not what she has; it's what she does," Annette declared. "She's been throwing herself at him."

Alone in the hall, Caroline's mouth dropped open. Throwing herself at him! Hadn't he been the one who invited her to La Maison Rouge after that first meeting? She hadn't asked him to take her to the touring production of *Cats*, either. Annette's accusation was ridiculous.

"Remember how anxious she was to help him with the food for the reception?" someone asked.

It wasn't fair! The girl was making it sound like Caroline had stolen the opportunity from the rest of them. No one else had wanted to lift a finger!

Caroline didn't recognize the next voice she heard. "And where was she during the reception? I didn't see her refilling any empty plates on the buffet table."

"Robert wasn't working around the buffet, either . . ."

"Didn't I tell you?" Annette squealed. "I saw them on the lawn after the reception."

"What?" the others said in unison.

"Are you sure?" Ellis asked. "I mean, if you saw them, why didn't you mention it earlier?"

If she could be glad about anything, Caroline was thankful her roommate was in the lounge bringing a little sanity to the ludicrous conversation.

"It was them," Annette said with assurance. "They were eating a chocolate-mousse pie."

Caroline had to wonder how Annette could possibly know what kind of pie they had been eating. She must have been awfully close. She quickly tried to remember what she and Robert had said on the lawn. Was there anything Annette could twist into some vicious lie?

"Chocolate-mousse pie?" The girls sounded

intrigued. "Is that his favorite or something?"

"How would she know what kind of pie he likes?"

"She must have found out somehow and then used it to entice him to go out on the lawn with her . . ." Annette made them sound absolutely wicked.

Caroline took a step forward, determined to crash into the room and set the facts straight. Robert had bought the pie. She hadn't set a trap for him.

"Then there was that night in Denver . . ."

The girls all squealed. "What night in Denver?"

"Last Friday night," someone explained. "A girl in my dorm saw them at *Cats*."

"So they went to a play," Caroline heard Ellis say, "I knew about it. I watched her get dressed. What's the big deal?"

"And when did she get home?"

"I don't know. I—"

"See?" Annette interrupted Ellis. Caroline wished Annette had let her roommate talk. She had cried herself to sleep before Ellis came home that night. Her roommate had found her in bed before midnight.

But Annette wasn't finished. "Just how far do you think this thing has gone?" she asked in a low voice. "Midnight meetings on the lawn? Overnight trips to Denver?"

"You're right," someone croaked. "Robert Winston wouldn't be dating a freshman unless she was making it worth his while."

"Are you saying she's been sleeping with him?" came a horrified voice.

The silence in the room was deafening to Caroline. When no one spoke, she could just imagine the smug, knowing looks being exchanged between the girls. And the worst thing was that Ellis didn't speak up. Her roommate wasn't doing anything to defend her.

Does Ellis believe Annette's fantasy? Caroline thought wildly. She couldn't They were living together, for heaven's sake. Her roommate was simply outnumbered—there were too many girls in the room determined to accuse Caroline of seducing Robert. Still, it hurt that she hadn't even tried.

"I have to get out of here!" she whispered aloud. What would she do if someone whipped around the corner and collided with her? She had never been so humiliated in her whole life. And she'd been embarrassed plenty of times around Chrissy, but nothing had been this awful.

How could she face those girls again? How could she sit in the same room tonight with Ellis, knowing that her roommate hadn't defended her? How could she ever see Robert again when those girls were spreading such horrible rumors about them both?

Caroline stumbled down the hall with her hands tangled in her long, blond hair. She had to find someone who could help her decide what to do. She could call her mother, but she would just get worried. She could try calling Luke, but how was she going to explain Robert to him? Who could help her?

". . . *à la bibliothèque*." Chrissy blew her bangs off her forehead. "I'm never going to get it right,"

"Sure you will," Denise promised. "Who cares if we're not going to speak French like the natives? Is either one of us going to marry some French guy and live in Paris?"

Chrissy giggled. "Probably not. I wouldn't understand him when he asked me to marry him!"

They both jumped when the door flew open. Chrissy started to get up from her desk, until she saw who was standing in the doorway.

"Chrissy. I've got to talk to you!" Caroline shouted.

Turning her back on her cousin, Chrissy asked, "What happened? Are Luke, Robert, and Joe all too busy for you?"

Caroline sniffed, "Maybe I deserve that and maybe I don't, but please let me come in."

"Hey, Chrissy," Denise said. "Your cousin doesn't look very good. Is it an emergency, Caroline?"

"A personal emergency," she replied.

Denise slapped her jeaned thigh. "I just remembered. I left my notebook in the biology lab. I'd better go find it before it gets lost."

"Isn't that your notebook on the floor?" Chrissy asked, but her roommate had already disappeared. Still keeping her back to her cousin, she asked, "What's so terrible about your life?"

She heard Caroline come into the room and sit on the lower bunk. "You know I love Luke."

"So you've mentioned . . ."

"He really is the most important guy—the only guy—in my life. But Robert is so charming."

Chrissy wanted to tell her cousin she didn't want to hear about her problems. Considering the absolute lack of guys in her life, she didn't want to hear how tough it was to have too many men.

"Robert and I have had a few good times together, but he and I didn't do anything that would hurt Luke."

Chrissy spun around in her chair. "Are you sure?"

Caroline started to cry again. "Not you, too, Chrissy. I thought you'd be on my side."

"You never wanted to see me again," Chrissy reminded her cousin. "Why should I be on your side?"

"But you didn't hear what they were saying . . ."

"Who? What are you talking about?" Chrissy was starting to get concerned. Caroline wasn't the kind of girl to lose it over little things. Something had happened to really upset her cousin, and she cared despite her angry feelings.

Caroline sniffed and dried the tears off her cheeks with her hands. "I had a good day, so I decided to drop by the lounge to see my friends. But when I got there, they were talking about me

. . . and Robert. They said I'd been chasing him. They said I'd been sl . . . sleeping with him—" Caroline broke down in a fit of sobs.

"Who's spreading these lies?" Chrissy jumped to her feet, ready to challenge anyone who would make up such stories about her cousin.

"Annette . . . and the others," she croaked.

Chrissy's mouth dropped open. "Your wonderful Music Society friends?"

"I *thought* they were my friends," Caroline said sadly.

"Why would they want to do this to you?" Chrissy couldn't imagine any reason they would want to attack her cousin.

"Jealousy." Caroline reached for a tissue and wiped her nose. "They'd all like to date Robert, but he's never asked any of them out."

"Did he ask you out?" Chrissy asked.

"I went to a play with him last weekend." Caroline put her hand out to stop Chrissy from speaking. "I know I shouldn't have gone because of Luke. But it doesn't mean I deserve to be treated this way."

"Of course it doesn't."

"You aren't mad about Luke?"

Chrissy looked at the dark smudges under her cousin's eyes. They were obviously the result of more than one sleepless night. "I think you've been hard enough on yourself."

Caroline shook her head. "I thought you might kick me out of your room. Thanks for listening Chrissy."

"I thought about slamming the door in your face," Chrissy admitted. "But I'm glad I didn't. We can't let those girls get away with their lies."

"What are you going to do? March into the lounge and demand an apology? It's hard to fight rumors."

"I guess you're right." If they strung a banner on Elmer Frame declaring Cara's innocence, it would do more to spread the rumor than to stop it.

"You can't know how much it helps just to know there is someone I can trust around here." Caroline sighed heavily.

Chrissy felt ashamed with herself for thinking that Joe was more important than her cousin. She threw her arms around Caroline. "Call me anytime. After all, family is family."

Chapter 18

Standing outside the small restaurant, Caroline knew she'd been right to meet Robert off campus. If he'd picked her up at the dorm, or if they had gone to The Rocky Mountain Club, someone might have seen them.

She peered in the front window and saw him waving from a table near the back of the coffee shop. Caroline made her way around the tables, sorry she had to tell him she couldn't see him again outside of the Music Society. And if it turned out that she had to leave the Music Society because of all the gossip about her, she wouldn't see him at all.

"My day is better already," he declared when he pulled out her chair.

Caroline felt guilty. His day wouldn't be going

so well by the time they left the restaurant.

"I've ordered tea for both of us since you said you weren't hungry. It should be here any minute."

"Thank you, Robert." Caroline just hoped the tea would settle her nervous stomach.

"I wanted to see you, because I have something to ask you in person," he said mysteriously. "How would you like to see Prince this weekend?"

"Prince?" She would never have thought Robert was a Prince fan.

He got a sheepish grin on his face. "I won two tickets in a call-in contest at KLLM."

She laughed so hard that she rocked back in her chair and people turned to stare at her. Maybe it was nerves, or maybe it was the hilarious picture in her mind of Robert calling the radio station. Whatever the reason, she laughed until her sides ached.

"If you ever recover from this attack of the giggles, I hope you'll give me an answer."

His words sobered her instantly. "I can't go with you," she said softly.

He pushed his glasses into place and peered at her. "You don't like Prince? I can certainly relate to that. We'll find something else to do."

"No, I can't," she said, staring down at her lap.

He started tapping on the table. "What's wrong? I thought we had a good time together last week."

"We did. But we can't do it again."

"Why not?"

Caroline had planned to mention the gossip going around the Music Society, but suddenly that didn't seem important. No one was going to repeat the stories to him. He would just feel sorry for her, and she didn't want his sympathy. The girls in the lounge weren't their real problem. "There's someone else . . ."

"Who? Not the big guy who wears plain flannel shirts?"

Joe? He thought she would turn him down because of Joe Thornton? When had he ever seen them together? If this situation wasn't so difficult to explain, it would be funny. "No, it's not him."

"Then I don't understand." He continued to tap out a steady rhythm on the tabletop.

"There's a guy I've known for quite a while."

"A boyfriend back home," he concluded.

"Not exactly. Luke is a neighbor of my cousin from Iowa. He's at the Air Force Academy now."

Robert folded his hands over his chest. "I see."

He sounded so disappointed that she had to ask, "Was I wrong to work on the reception with you? Was it wrong for us to go to the play together?"

"Those are questions you have to answer, Cara." He wasn't going to help her out. "Were you thinking about your cadet when we gorged ourselves on chocolate-mousse pie on the lawn? Who were you kissing on Fielding Hall's porch?"

"I was kissing you," she said. Caroline wanted him to know she hadn't been pretending he was

Luke. "That's what makes this all so confusing. Maybe we should never have been together."

"But we were. And I enjoy myself whenever I'm with you."

"I like being with you, too, Robert. But it's wrong, so we can't do it anymore."

He reached for her hand. When she tried to avoid his touch, he grabbed her wrist and held if tightly. "Don't be so definite. Things can change."

"You mean my boyfriend might not want me anymore?" If Luke dumped her, she was going to have a list of people to call. First Joe, and now Robert.

"He'd be a fool to let you go, but some men can be very foolish when it comes to women," he told her. "I'm not asking for any promises. I'm just asking you not to say we can *never* be together again."

"That's fair," she said uncertainly. The odds on them getting together were pretty remote, but she liked the idea of ending things on a friendly basis.

"It's not that easy," he said as the tea arrived. "What am I going to do with two Prince tickets?"

He sounded so dejected she almost suggested that they attend the concert as a sort of farewell. But that wouldn't be fair to him or to Luke. *How come I'm so unsure about what I want*? Caroline asked herself. *Life was so much less complicated in high school!*

Ringgg . . .

Chrissy blindly reached out for the blaring alarm clock next to her pillow, trying to turn off the buzzer. When it didn't stop she opened one eye. Her glow-in-the-dark clock said two A.M.

Ringgg . . .

"Answer the phone," Denise mumbled from the lower bunk.

"You do it," said Chrissy "I'm up here." If she tried to jump down when she was still half-asleep, she'd probably fall and break her neck.

"Hello?" Denise muttered. "It's for you."

Her roommate stretched the receiver toward the top bunk. Chrissy hung over the edge of her bed and grabbed the phone.

"Hello?

"Hi, Chrissy! Were you sleeping?" Caroline asked in an animated voice.

"Yeah." She wasn't thinking fast enough to come up with a polite lie.

"Sorry, but I can't sleep. Can you come over and talk?"

"At two in the morning?"

"I really need you," Caroline claimed. "Everything is so confusing. I have to talk to someone."

"And who else could you call in the middle of the night?" Chrissy wasn't thrilled Caroline had chosen her, but she had encouraged her cousin to call *anytime*.

"You're the only one who'll understand," Caroline insisted.

"Okay. I'll try to hurry," Chrissy groaned.

Five minutes later she was walking up the steps to Fielding Hall, tugging her sweat-shirt bottom over her hips and the top of her jeans and wondering why she hadn't asked Caroline over to Culver Hall. Caroline was waiting inside the door.

"We can talk in the living room," Caroline said.

They settled in the opposite ends of a loveseat, curling their feet beneath them. Caroline smoothed her robe over her legs. "College isn't quite what I expected it to be."

"We've only been here four weeks. Give it a chance," Chrissy advised. In the last few days, she'd discovered it was much easier to look into the future than to dwell on her less than successful past.

"There's so much studying to do. And there are so many people . . ."

Chrissy flinched at the memory of some of the people she had met. Instead of Denise or Nan, Joe came to mind first. Although she fought it, memories of meeting and losing Joe flashed through her mind.

"You're thinking about Joe," Caroline observed.

"I can't help it sometimes," Chrissy said despondently.

"You know I really hoped it would work out between you two."

Chrissy pointed to her head. "In here, I know he never liked me the way I like him. Logically, I know you didn't steal him away from me—"

"But you feel differently here." Caroline

thumped a hand in the area near her heart.

"I guess it really doesn't matter who was wrong, or if anyone was wrong. Joe's still gone."

"And I'm still you're favorite cousin," Caroline said sweetly.

"And my friend," Chrissy finished. "If anything, we've learned never to doubt that ever again."

Caroline stared at her for a minute and then shook her head. "No way. Just please, don't send me back up Elmer Frame."

They sat in a silence for a while. Chrissy realized Caroline was trying to sort out her thoughts and she simply needed some company. She tried hard to stay awake.

Finally, Caroline said, "I talked to Robert tonight. I told him I couldn't see him this weekend."

"Was it hard?"

"Yes." Caroline stared at the ceiling. "Talking with him, I realized how much I liked being with him. But I can't forget about Luke."

"What can I do to help you?" Chrissy asked, hoping Caroline would invite her to spend the night.

Caroline ran her hand through her hair. "I don't know. I just don't want to have to face anyone for a few days. Maybe I can hide out somewhere."

"Or maybe we could go somewhere . . ." Chrissy said slowly, a smile creeping onto her sleepy features.

They jumped up at the same time. "Luke!"

"I promised I'd visit him," Caroline said, her eyes dancing.

"And my luck should improve with all those men around!" Chrissy cried. "But don't you have tons of work?"

"Sure. But I can do it Sunday night," Caroline said, conveniently forgetting how long the work would take.

"I don't have any classes after noon tomorrow," Chrissy realized. "What about you?"

"Friday?" She thought for a minute. "I have the afternoon off, too!"

"We can be in Fort Collins by dinnertime!"

Caroline raised her hand. "We have to check with Luke first!"

They raced to the bank of pay phones. Caroline dug her hands in to her robe pockets. "I don't have any money. What about you?"

Chrissy could only find a quarter.

"I can charge the call to my parents credit card," Caroline said. "After all, this is an emergency."

The call went through quickly. Caroline clutched the receiver to her ear. "I think I can hear him coming down the hall." She held her breath for a moment. "Luke? Is that you? It's me Cara."

Chrissy was dying to know what he was saying. Her fingers were crossed on both hands. He had to have a free weekend. If he was too busy to see them, she was going to scream and wake up every person in Fielding Hall.

"Tell me the news," she whispered in Caroline's free ear until her cousin put her hand over it.

"That's right, we want to visit this weekend. We can leave tomorrow afternoon." Caroline paused to listen again. "Yes. Both Chrissy and me."

What if he doesn't want me to come along? Chrissy worried. While Caroline escaped the campus and her problems, she would be left here with Ellis and all those Music Society people lurking around, telling their lies. If she saw one of them, she could not be held responsible for her actions. To prevent herself from doing anything rash, Chrissy needed to get off campus and cool down.

She grabbed Caroline's arm and tugged on it. "Can I go, too?"

Caroline nodded and said into the phone, "We're not sure about the bus schedule. This came up kind of quickly."

Chrissy tried to grab Caroline's arm again, but Caroline backed away in an effort to concentrate. Determined to get her cousin's attention, Chrissy jumped up and down in front of her.

Finally Caroline rested the receiver on her shoulder. "What is it?"

"Ask him if he has any friends for me." Chrissy rubbed her hands together in anticipation.

"Luke, can you find Chrissy a date?" She smiled at Luke's response. "Let's just say things have been a little bumpy here at Colorado U."

Chrissy paced until Caroline hung up the

phone. Then she grabbed her cousin by the shoulders. "Tell me everything."

"After our last classes tomorrow, we'll skip lunch in the deadly dining hall and catch a bus. Luke will find some way to meet us at the station."

Chrissy threw back her head and was ready to howl when Caroline clapped a hand over her mouth.

"It's three o'clock in the morning. Promise me you won't scream." When her cousin nodded, Caroline removed her hand.

Chrissy was too excited to stand still. "Fort Collins, here we come! I hope the Air Force Academy is ready for us!"

Here's a sneak preview of *Road Trip,* book number eighteen in the continuing SUGAR & SPICE series from Ivy Books:

How do I get myself into these messes? Chrissy wondered as the Futura I rolled out of the hangar and onto the runway—with her inside! The plane steadily gained speed, and Chrissy sat down quickly and fumbled with the safety strap. *Holy mazoley,* Chrissy thought, *I'm a stowaway!* This was the last thing she'd expected to happen when she'd decided to take a peek inside the experimental aircraft.

She gazed out the window at the airfield, now just a blur of people and planes and hangars. Without warning, Chrissy felt the supersonic jet leave the ground.

She looked out the window and gasped. There they were—the Rocky Mountains. It seemed as if they were only a few feet away as the plane whizzed over the snow-capped peaks. Chrissy sighed in disappointment as the plane eventually veered away from the mountains and headed back in the direction of the airfield.

But as she started to lean forward to get a better view of the retreating peaks, Chrissy was suddenly thrown back against the seat. The force pushing against her was so strong, she couldn't move.

It was no use. She couldn't block out the tremendous weight of the force pulling her down. Despite her discomfort, Chrissy noticed that the plane was losing speed as it continued to gain altitude.

The engines aren't working. This is the end, she thought in despair. *Eighteen years—it's been short, but sweet. Chrissy Madden is history now.*

Chrissy kept her eyes squeezed tightly shut and clenched the armrests, waiting for the inevitable crash. But instead, the force subsided and within moments she was able to move freely. She opened her eyes and looked around. Miraculously, she was still in one piece, and so, apparently, was the plane, which was now flying straight and level as if nothing had happened. Chrissy felt like cheering. Then the cockpit door opened and one of the officers was walking toward her. His stern, weathered face was a pinkish red color, and his eyes were bulging in disbelief.

"Where the heck did you come from?" he bellowed.

Chrissy just stared at him.

"If you're not going to answer, at least get your hand off the call button," he ordered sharply.

Chrissy looked down at her hand and realized that as she was clutching the armrest, she was also pressing a button that must have sounded in the cockpit.

"I'm glad to see you can listen to orders," the officer snapped. "But I'm afraid it won't do you much good now. You are in very serious trouble, young lady."

ABOUT THE AUTHOR

Janet Quin-Harkin is the author of more than forty books for young adults, including the best-selling *Ten-Boy Summer* and *On Our Own*, its sequel series. Ms. Quin-Harkin lives just outside of San Francisco with her husband, three teenage daughters, and one son.